P9-DMF-617

From the Files of
Madison Finn

Read all the books about Madison Finn!

#1 Only the Lonely
#2 Boy, Oh Boy!

Coming Soon!

#3 Play It Again

From the Files of

Madison Finn

Only the Lonely

HYPERION
New York

 For information address Hyperion Books for Children, 114 Fifth Avenue, New York, New York 10011-5690.

Printed in the United States of America

First Edition
7 9 10 8

The main body of text of this book is set in 13-point Frutiger Roman.

ISBN 0-7868-1553-1

Visit www.madisonfinn.com

For Mom with love—always remember MTM,
sour cream & onion chips, and
Warren Avenue

Special thanks to my editor, Helen Perelman

Chapter 1

"Hnnnnnnugh! WHAT is your problem?" Madison grunted at her new orange laptop computer. She was smack-dab in the middle of downloading a picture of a super-cute *Ursus maritimus* (a.k.a. polar bear) when the screen just froze.

She knew her hard drive had plenty of memory.

She punched all the right keys.

But nothing.

Sometimes in the past, Madison's computer screen would freeze, but only for a blip. This was different. The computer wasn't *really* the one with a problem. Right now, Madison was frozen, too.

Madison Francesca Finn had a dreadful case of late-summer brain freeze. It was not the kind of

brain freeze you get when you drink a Grape Slurpee too fast. This was the kind of brain freeze that happens when your thoughts get stuck in a whirly swirl of loneliness, friendlessness, and total and utter boredom. This was the chronic, moronic, pain-in-the-brain freeze that happens when everyone you know is at camp but you're stuck at home with Mom; the summer reading list you were supposed to be finishing up hasn't even been *unfolded*; and you have no pool options on 95° days.

"Yikes!" Madison yelped, jumping up from her desk chair. "Why is it doing this to me, Phin?" She glared at her dog, Phineas T. Finn, who was curled up next to a giant metal file cabinet in the corner of her bedroom.

He poked up his wrinkly nose into the air and sneezed. "Rowroooooooo!" This pug hated it when his nap was interrupted.

"Well, I'll just restart it just to be sure everything's okay," Madison said out loud, groaning and hitting a few special keys, a trick her dad had taught her.

Dad was the one who had computerized Madison in the first place. He had shown her what DSL and HTML meant before most of her classmates even knew they even existed. He loved computer jokes, too, even though he told the same ones more than once.

"Hey, Maddie, why did the Net chick cross the road?" he would ask.

"I dunno, Dad . . . why?" Madison would say with pretend interest, even if it was the third time she'd heard it.

"To get ONLINE!" Dad would laugh.

And that was one of his better jokes.

Just this year, her parents had bought this new laptop in Madison's favorite color, along with a mega-pack of disks, special desktop-publishing software, and a slightly used scanner. Mom had crooned, "It'll be a great way to organize your thoughts, honey bear," as they unpacked the computer back in May. "Just think, you're on the cutting edge of technology. This fall, you'll be the smartest seventh grader at Far Hills."

Madison thought her Mom wanted her to be a computer genius or a writing genius or anyone who had "genius" potential. Madison didn't exactly feel like a "genius" *yet*, but she did know her way around a computer, especially on the Internet.

The computer beeped and zinged, and Madison's desktop page appeared once again. The polar bear was there in a document marked "recovered," and the desktop reappeared as a collage of white rhinos and mountain gorillas.

Madison always used pictures of endangered animals as her screen savers. In fact, she considered herself an official animal advocate both on the computer and off. She fantasized about working for the *National Geographic Explorer* TV show, or becoming

a super vet, or maybe even becoming a documentary filmmaker like her mom.

With her computer unfrozen and ready to go, Madison logged on to bigfishbowl.com. Usually a chat room helped her break through a case of brain freeze better than most things. She knew meeting new people online wasn't the same as having actual, in-the-same-room friends whose hair you could braid or who could play hoops, but it gave her someone to talk to.

She'd logged on for the first time a year ago with Mom's permission. The people in charge of the site were sticklers for safety.

Madison's chat room screen name was "MadFinn," which was pretty funny, considering she was a "Finn" among the fishes, so to speak. Most of the people inside bigfishbowl.com were girls talking about girl stuff. Madison loved the way the home page looked like a real fishbowl, with seaweed, and even orange fish. She clicked on a rainbow fish to get into the Main Fishbowl, the waiting room where kids picked the chat they wanted to join. Madison scanned the list.

```
I am sooo bored! Hello!
(32 fish)

Tell me anything u want GRRRLS ONLY
(12 fish)
```

****animal lovers here*****
(3 fish)

Private! Wanna be keypals?
(28 fish)

Pictures of cute boyz can u help me
(11 fish)

only the lonely
(1 fish)

Madison picked "animal lovers here" and went inside. She was sure she must be in the right place. Maybe she'd meet a fellow polar bear admirer?

<Crazygal>: That is kool beans
MadFinn has entered the room.
<Crazygal>: Hiya!!!!!!
<Wayout>: Madfinn stats?
<MadFinn>: Hell
<MadFinn>: ooooo Hellooooo
<Iluvcats>: How r u? I love cats.
<MadFinn>: stats f/12/NY u?
<Crazygal>: f/14/DE
<MadFinn>: hey cats I love animals too.
<Iluvcats>: I LOVE CATS!!!
<Wayout>: :>) I loooove Jimmie J!!!!
<MadFinn>: Do you have cats?
<Crazygal>: GMTA I like Downtown Boyz 2!

Downtown Boyz was an all-guy singing group whose lead singer Jimmie J was pretty cute but . . . *wait a minute!* Madison wanted to talk about animals. This was the "animal lovers here" room. Why were they changing the subject? Who cared about Jimmie J? And why wasn't Iluvcats girl responding?

```
<Wayout>: (( )) :* they r sooooooo
   hot
<Crazygal>: IMO Jimmie is the
   hottest :-@
Iluvcats has left the room.
```

As soon as cat girl left the room, Madison left, too.

She went back to the room list in search of *someone* who would talk about animals or computers or something besides Jimmie J. She saw one other room that looked semi-interesting.

```
only the lonely (1 fish)
```

That was *exactly* how Madison felt. She missed her best friend, Aimee, who was away at ballet camp twirling around; and Egg, who was away at computer camp URL-ing around.

She clicked on "lonely" and hoped for the best.

Of course as luck would have it (and Madison's luck usually ran a little *sloooooow* these days), she entered and introduced herself with a quick "MadFinn" hello, but then nothing happened.

There was no "hello" back.

There was no "how r u?"

There was nothing. Madison waited almost three whole minutes before the "(1 fish)" responded in any way at all.

<Bigwheels>: ohhhh whoa i thought I was alone. My
<Bigwheels>: screen froze the computer is
<MadFinn>: helllooo????
<Bigwheels>: wicked slow sorry
<MadFinn>: u r not alone! i saw how r u?
<Bigwheels>: ok. How are
<MadFinn>: how old r u?
<Bigwheels>: 12 and yoo?
<MadFinn>: 12
<Bigwheels>: my birthday was last wk
<MadFinn>: (:o!!!! no way! happy birthday!
<Bigwheels>: thank you where do u live?
<MadFinn>: NY are you at camp?
<Bigwheels>: no. I'm at home washington state
<MadFinn>: omigod you are all the way across the
<MadFinn>: country that is so cool WOW

<Bigwheels>: yeah but I'm lonely here u know???
<MadFinn>: me too
<MadFinn>: and bored too
<Bigwheels>: wanna be keypals?
<MadFinn>: ok what's that?
<Bigwheels>: like penpals only email like
<MadFinn>: o ok. What is your email?
<Bigwheels>: send me your em
<MadFinn>: tell me your email and I will write 2 u

Madison waited.

<MadFinn>: tell me your email and I will write u!!!

Madison waited a little longer.

<MadFinn>: r u there?
<MadFinn>: Hellllloooooo?????
<Bigwheels>: *poof*

Poof?

Madison felt even *more* alone than when she had logged on, so of course she logged off immediately. She wasn't in the mood to be lonely anymore.

After that chat room fiasco, Madison went into her

super-special computer files. She accessed the files with a super-special password which was so super-special that even *she* forgot it sometimes. She had it taped inside the top drawer of her desk.

In the last few weeks (partly out of boredom and partly out of a desire to get her life together), Madison had begun a new system of personal information storage on the new computer.

She had been collecting magazine clippings like a pack rat for months. She'd stored them in multicolored rainbow folders up until now, but at last she was ready to load them online. Slowly, she was becoming computerized byte by byte.

The old scanner worked well, even if blue printed out more like purple. Dad said he'd eventually help her download more fun gifs from Web sites and teach her how to adjust the pixels properly, whatever those were. Madison was learning as fast as she could. In fact, she was certain she'd have her own Web page or even her own Web site one day. Maybe she'd be a Web site *genius*? Mom would love that.

In addition to downloading, scanning, and saving, Madison decided she would *also* keep an online record of her most important feelings and most important thoughts. Of course, most people would have called something like this a "journal," but Madison thought that sounded way too obvious. She briefly considered calling her writing a "diary," too, but that was just as obvious so she called it

instead: *The Files of Madison Finn*.

She had friend files. She had homework files. She had nothing-in-particular files. She classified, collected, controlled, and computed *everything*. Here, inside this delightful orange computer, Madison was in the process of creating password-protected *miles* of files.

She opened one.

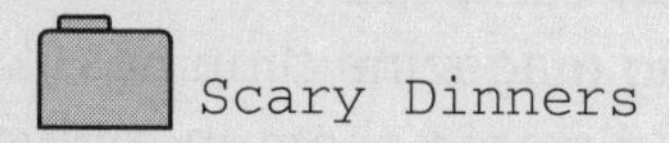

That made her laugh. On the screen before her was a graph on which Madison had plotted Mom's predictable fast-food dinners. After sixteen straight nights in a row of egg rolls, tacos, fried chicken, and other "scary" dinners, Madison was inspired to keep track. As of tonight, the graph showed pizza running neck and neck with Chinese food, with PB-&-J sandwiches lagging behind.

Tonight, Madison decided to open a brand new file in honor of her hour on bigfishbowl.com. She wondered what had happened to "Bigwheels" and why "Iluvcats" had just disappeared. Was it something she'd said?

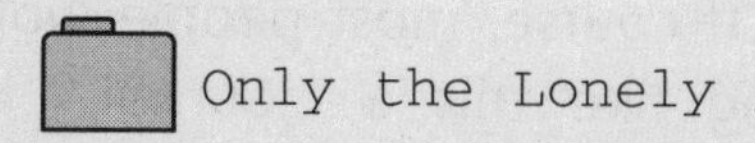

Madison closed her eyes for a second. She hoped in her heart of hearts that she'd get a hundred e-mails tomorrow. She longed for the speedy return

of Aimee and Egg. She secretly wished that even Daddy would come home again.

Is absolutely everyone having a good summer except for me? I mean I went to Brazil for a nature documentary film location scout with Mom. Ever since she started working for Budge Films she makes nature shows. We saw lots of weird-looking tree frogs there. They were slimy and the truth is I was sicker than sick of the frogs and fast food and planes and strangers, especially strangers.

I wish Aimee and Egg were right here, right now, right away. I wish I had a brother or sister. I wish I wasn't only the lonely. I wish seventh grade would just start already. Of course, I probably won't be able to deal with the change. I never have before.

Rude Awakening: I'm allergic to change.

I mean, I know I'm allergic to pollen, grasses, and mold spores. But change makes me break out into big hives. Just the thought of seventh grade gave me a giant pink welt right here on my shoulder. *Gross.*

Last summer after fifth grade Aimee and Egg were not far away at stupid camp. They were here with me, dancing in the sprinklers on Aimee's lawn like we did every summer, getting cooled off, and laughing like we did every summer. We were laughing really hard about some things I can't remember but

I know they were great. I know we ate all the Dreamsicles we wanted and we watched scary old movies like *The Mummy*.

Not this summer.

Mom would probably say that at least it's a good thing that I've identified my bizarre allergy and maybe it just doesn't matter if I fix it right now. All that matters is acknowledging it, right? The rest is just details, right? Mom says that we learn things in steps. So this is just step number one, I guess. This is just step number one in learning about life.

Lucky me.

I can't wait for step number two.

The cursor blinked on the empty space. Madison stopped and stared at what she'd written so far. The screen went black.

It was frozen *again*.

Madison leaned down to scratch the top of Phin's head.

So what if the screen was stuck! Madison decided she just didn't care if she got the "safe to turn off your computer" message or not. She just pressed the power button and walked away.

As she turned, Madison crashed into a purple blow-up chair in the middle of the room. It squeaked as she landed on her backside.

She plucked open the little plastic thingie that kept air in the chair. *Psssssssssssss*.

She capped it again quickly.

Could Madison Finn really ever be saved from loneliness?

"Madison!" Mom yelled from downstairs.

It was time to go to bed. As she stood up, Madison lost her balance and fell backward. She groaned.

She wanted her friends, but thanks to camp they were gone.

She wanted her Dad, but thanks to the divorce he was gone.

How could she ever handle a switch into seventh grade when she kept slipping *backward*?

"Rowroooo!" Phin growled. He could always tell when Madison was upset.

She pulled her body up and into the bathroom, but her brain was stuck in REWIND. She wished she could just press FAST FORWARD and get through this moment.

At this point, Madison Finn wasn't sure she could survive the end of the summer, let alone the beginning of a new school year.

Chapter 2

The next morning, Madison woke up to wet kisses from Phin. Smelly kisses of course. Dog breath.

"Oh, gross. Phin get off! Yeah, I love you, too." Madison gazed into his brown pug eyes. "Are you trying to tell me something, dog? Like W-A-L-K maybe?"

Phin danced on his back paws, jumping at the bed. Even Phin knew how to spell.

Madison wanted to lollygag around, but nature was calling—calling Phin, anyway. She pulled off her orange polka-dotted pajamas and slipped into short overalls so she and Phin could make a quick trip around the block.

Morning walks with Phin were the easiest. Madison walked out the porch door, down the

corner to Grove Street, up a few more streets, and then around the block to the intersection before turning back home.

But for some reason this morning, Phin was being difficult. He wouldn't pee, so Madison took a detour onto Ridge Road, the scenic route.

It smelled like honeysuckle. Phin's nose started sniffing a mile a minute. Madison's eyes scanned the neighborhood. Everything looked different here from the way she remembered. She even saw a new-looking green house where the old Martin family had lived for years. Everyone thought that house was haunted. But today it was a whole new house, freshly painted and all.

Just as Madison was staring at the green house, a young girl walked out onto its front steps.

Madison kept staring.

The girl stared straight back.

Madison stared some more and she kept smiling—it was easy to be friendly at a distance. After a moment, however, the girl started to walk toward her. That's when Madison panicked. It was never as easy to be friendly up close. She felt the urge to run.

Madison wasn't quite sure where she was running *to*, but she sure knew how to run. She could have dashed away from that green house lickety-split too if it hadn't been for Phin, who tugged her right back to where she had started.

"Hi!" the stranger said, cheerfully. She walked right up to Madison and Phin on the sidewalk. "I'm Fiona. Do you live around here?"

Madison managed a feeble "Uh-huh," in response.

"Oh cool, do you live on Ridge Road?" Fiona asked.

"I live . . . uh . . ." Madison pointed behind her, in the general direction of Blueberry Street. It wasn't her most eloquent moment of all time.

Suddenly a woman called out from the door of the green house. "Fiona! Let's go, young lady!"

"Yeeps!" The girl smiled at Madison. "I gotta run! See you around the neighborhood?" She disappeared again up the path, almost as quietly as she'd appeared, waving the whole way. "Nice to meet you—sort of!"

Madison waved too. Then she waited a moment to see if the girl would reappear, but no one came outside. Madison stared at the big brown duck painted on the side of the family's mailbox and read the swirly letters: THE WATERS FAMILY.

As she and Phin made tracks back home to 5 Blueberry Street, Madison wondered when she would see Fiona again.

"Rowroooo!" Phin agreed.

As soon as they arrived home, Madison and Phin noticed an icky-sticky charred smell coming from the kitchen. The pug's nose was sniffing wildly at the air.

"Mom?" Madison hurried inside. "Is something burning?"

She stopped dead in her tracks. Had someone stolen Fast Food Mother in the middle of the night and replaced her with Cook-Me-Breakfast Mother? Mom was cooking? She was even wearing a tacky "Kiss the Cook" apron.

"Have a seat!" Mom announced, shoving a plate of very yellow scrambled eggs and very burned toast in front of Madison.

It was the morning of surprises.

"Gee, Mom," Madison said, a little stunned by the greeting, and the smell. Then she added, "They seem a little, well . . . gold, actually. What's up with that?"

Madison knew what was really up; Mom had forgotten to add milk again. One time Mom had tried to make lasagna, which came out more like red soup, but Madison had just slurped and said nothing. Madison didn't see the point in hurting Mom's feelings just because her pasta was a little runny.

Mom beamed. "Sweetie, today is a special day just for you and so I thought breakfast was a good way to start off. What do you think? Today we can go over to the Far Hills Shoppes and get you some new clothes for seventh grade. I know starting junior high is a big deal and I know I have been away a lot on business lately and, well, won't it be nice to spend a little time together?"

Usually Madison was good at predicting Mom's sudden bursts of "nice." But not this morning.

"Come on. What gives, Mom?" Madison laughed. "What's the catch?"

"Catch? There is no catch. Don't you *want* to go shopping?" Mom asked.

Madison scooped up a forkful of food and nodded. She would have said something, but she didn't want to gag on the eggs.

As soon as they'd cleared away the breakfast dishes, Madison filled Phin's water dish and waited for Mom to put on her eyeliner, lipstick, and concealer. That usually took a while, so Madison visited her computer keyboard in the meantime. She could check her e-mail, at least.

There was no mail. Madison was discouraged. She sighed, opened a new file folder, and began to type.

Met this new girl over on Ridge Road. She looked like the singer Brandy, like with long braids and cool clothes. Her name is Fiona Waters and she was very friendly and I think she wanted to be my friend. Is that possible? She looked my age and she must have just moved in because I know the house she lives in. Way, way long ago this other family the Martins lived there.

I wonder what happened to the Martins?

How can people just suddenly disappear and then appear in the neighborhood from out of nowhere? Everything really does change when you aren't paying attention.

I of course clammed up the minute Fiona said "hi" because I am useless around strangers. I wanted to run away. It's like I had the words to talk right here on the tip of my tongue, but no luck. I'm stuck. Sometimes I think there's this master conspiracy to keep me tongue-tied and friendless, for the rest of the summer. I wish Aimee would just come home, already!

At least I have Phinnie.

On their way out the door, Madison asked Mom if she would please drive to the Far Hill Shoppes via Ridge Road. She wanted to drive past the green house again, of course. As they passed, Madison saw that the Waters family car was no longer parked in the driveway. Fiona had vanished.

Madison and her mom cruised over a few blocks to the back entrance of the mall. There was a sign draped across the storefront: GOING-OUT-OF-BUSINESS BACK-TO-SCHOOL EXTRA-SPECIAL SUPER-SALE. Sales always sounded great to Mom, so that's where they started.

While Madison loaded her arms with cotton tees, embroidered khakis, and sweaters, Mom remained attached to her cell phone, waiting on a bench by the cash register. Some producer or director was always calling her about something.

"Mom, can I get these? Please?" Madison pleaded gently, trying to distract Mom from the phone. She held out a few shirts for Mom's vote. This was supposed to be *their* day together, after all.

"Well, try them on first, I wanna see," Mom said, grabbing a tank top out of the pile. She took the phone away from her mouth and frowned. "I don't know about shirts like *this* one, sweetie. People will be staring, don't you think?"

"Staring?" Madison suddenly felt self-conscious. Staring at *what*? Madison hardly had any boobs yet. She quickly gave Mom an "I could die right here, right now, if you ever, ever, *ever* refer to my chest again" look. She'd show Mom some *staring*.

Of course, Mom never noticed Madison's stares. She was too busy getting right back onto her cell phone or doing some work thing.

Madison pouted a little and proceeded into the dressing room. She felt hot with that special kind of embarrassment you only get when you're out with your mom. She felt hot from carrying all these stupid clothes. She felt—

Wham! She felt awful! She had walked right into someone on the way into the dressing area.

"Yikes!" Madison blurted out. "Are you okay?"

"Excuse me, I am so sorry," the girl said, suddenly bursting into a wide grin. "Hey, don't I know you?"

Madison's jaw slackened. It was Fiona. She was wearing the same yellow sundress Madison had seen

her in earlier. Madison noticed Fiona's toenails were painted a perfect grape color and she had on an equally perfect pair of yellow jelly sandals. Madison had always wanted sandals like those.

Although she had an uncanny ability to process many visual details in a very short period of time, speaking was something Madison wasn't so quick about.

"H-h-howdy!" Madison stuttered. *Howdy?* Her cheeks turned the color of cherry tomatoes. *Howdy?*

"Hey, you were the one I met this morning, right? With your dog. He was cute." Fiona smiled again. "What's *your* name again?"

"Madison," she mumbled.

Fiona kept smiling. "I'm Fiona, but I think I told you that already, right? I'm new in Far Hills."

"Uh-huh," said Madison, listening. "New."

"Well, new because we just moved here and I don't actually know anyone here in Far Hills yet except my brother, Chet, he's my twin brother, so he doesn't count obviously as a friend-friend because he's not a girl and . . ." her voice trailed off.

She was good at talking—*a lot*.

"By the way, do people call you Madison or Maddie?"

"Most people call me Madison. Except my friends. They call me Maddie. But you can call me something else. . . . You can call me a complete moron for acting so dumb this morning."

Fiona chuckled. "You're funny! And you are so not a moron! I'm so happy to meet you. I was beginning to think I wouldn't have any new friends at all this summer and it can get pretty lonely around here, you know what I mean? It's like the whole world is away at camp or something."

Madison sighed again. The embarrassment of the previous seven minutes and twelve seconds started to wear off.

Fiona was pretty *and* she was so nice.

Fiona was even a little lonely.

Was Fiona Waters just like Madison Finn?

They cruised around the sweater racks and Fiona picked out a speckled blue cardigan while Madison grabbed an orange sweater set. In the blink of an eye a day of shopping was reduced to good-byes, the exchange of phone numbers and e-mail addresses, and a word or two about junior high jitters.

"So I'll see ya!" Fiona said as she walked out of the store with her mom.

Madison grinned. She wasn't so afraid to smile up close anymore.

On their way out of the mall, Madison and her mom stopped for banana splits. A little hot fudge goes a long way, especially when you've been shopping all day. Just the thought of seventh grade made Madison crave sweets. She knew that meant risking a zit, but today it was a risk she was willing to take.

In between bites Mom asked, "So who was that

girl you were talking to in the store?"

"I met her when I was trying stuff on." Madison volunteered the details of the dressing-room collision and Fiona and her twin brother and whatever else she could remember. "They live on Ridge Road."

"You know, Olga told me a new family had moved into the old Martin house." Olga was a real-estate broker friend who kept Mom in the neighborhood gossip loop. "Was she nice?" Mom asked.

"She's *really* nice, Mom. Is that weird?" Madison answered her own question. "Well, I'm a weird magnet, so it all makes sense."

"You are *not* weird, honey! You're perfect," Mom said. "I'm sure Fiona is going to be a wonderful new friend. That's how things happen, when you least expect them."

When they got home, Madison checked her e-mail right away. It *was* the day of surprises, after all. She had mail.

```
From: Eggaway
To: MadFinn
Subject: hi
Date: Wed, 23 Aug 3:21 PM
```

```
Hey Madison, whassup? Hey computer
camp rocks so much I don't want
2come back 2 stupid Far Hills! i
cant believe 7th grade is here in
like a min. Hey anyway I miss yor
stupid dog Phin. LOL!!! Is he still
```

FAT? I think you and me should defniteley take that cmpter class together in school by thewaynow that you have this ok talk L8R. Drew says hi BTW. Write back BYE!!!

Madison smiled. Egg was one of her best friends in the entire universe and she really missed him—*and* his stupid spelling mistakes. He didn't care about letters much; he was more of a numbers kind of guy. She liked that, of course. The funniest thing about Egg was how he had gotten his nickname. He didn't get it because he was a brain, although he *was*. When he was six, Egg got hit by a raw egg on Halloween. (He had the scar to prove it.) Egg's "real" name was Walter Emilio Diaz.

Madison clicked on REPLY.

From: MadFinn
To: Eggaway
Subject: Re:hi
Date: Wed, 23 Aug 5:05 PM

Egg it is sooooo good to hear from you!!!

How is computer camp? Do you have any other new friends? How is Drew? What else is new? I am here in Far Hills by myself (with Phin and Mom).

When are you coming home? Aimee is coming back next week. I hope I see you soon! TTFN

Madison clicked SEND, smiling. She hoped her friend missed her just as much as she missed him.

The next e-mail was from Dad.

From: jefffinn
To: MadFinn
Subject: I'M COMING HOME!
Date: Wed, 23 Aug 4:40 PM

Hey sweetheart.

I am coming back begin. next wk. Let's dinner?

I'll make you good food! Tell your mother. I will call w/dates.

I love you, Daddy

p.s. got you a present! Call me xoxoxo ;>)

Madison grinned at the little hugs and kisses and the winky symbol. Daddy always sent those.

No more mail. Madison looked at her list of files. She opened the Fiona file.

So does this mean the stars are aligned for me? Two meetings out of the blue with

the new girl. I believe in coincidences.

I wish I had hair like hers, it is so shiny even in those braids. She just moved here from California and I think she looks a little like a model actually. I don't know. She has eyes that are a smoky green color and that is why I think she looks like a model. She was really nice to me even though I was acting so bizarre.

I hope she doesn't think I am the biggest loser for trying to run away this morning or for having like nothing interesting to say. I helped her pick out clothes for school. She actually asked me my opinion. No one ever does that.

I guess the reason I am acting all worried is because deep down I would like her to be my friend.

The moment Madison wrote the words "deep down I would like her to be my friend," she started over-thinking.

Dad always teased Madison about "over-thoughts." She would get one idea and then think about it over and over and over until she was completely muddled. Madison couldn't believe how much missing her friends was messing with her head. Egg was coming back soon. Aimee was coming home soon. She had to get ready to go back to everything the way it was before the summer started.

Now she had one guilty over-thought that would not go away.

If I want to be friends with someone new, does that mean that there's something wrong with me and my old friends?

Dad's voice echoed, "Don't over-think it, honey. Just let things be."

But it was too late.

Madison Finn had already way over-*thunk*.

Chapter 3

Madison bolted up in bed. She was in the middle of a hazy, crazy nightmare about ice cream, orange sweater sets, and school. She was walking into the Far Hills auditorium followed by a hundred drooling pugs and tree frogs all barking and croaking the same thing because in this dream, Madison could understand the language of animals, of course.

"Rowroo! Ribbut!" This meant: keep away from Madison Finn!

Madison knew she had a good imagination, but this was ridiculous. She turned on her laptop. The monitor glowed in the half-dark of her bedroom.

Dreams

I'm being chased by Phin clones and tree frogs like the ones Mom and I saw in Brazil! Maybe I shouldn't have had those cookies before bed? Mom told me I could get weird thoughts from sweet stuff too close to bedtime.

I think I am definitely weird.

Who dreams about dogs and frogs?

"Don't over-think it, honey. Just—"

Madison decided to "let things be" in an early morning bubbly tub. Mom had all these cool aromatherapy bubble baths and Madison loved the way they made the room and her skin smell. She couldn't believe that there had been a time in third grade when she didn't want to take a bath or wash her hair. Things had really changed since then.

Madison looked down in the bath water and traced the shape of her own body. Her shape was changing a lot these days, too—and it felt weird. Her hips were bigger. She grabbed at the fleshy parts of herself to see if they'd grown or shrunk.

Madison rubbed her hand across her shin. It was fuzzy. Had it always been this way?

"Good morning," Mom said all of a sudden, kicking open the bathroom door unannounced, arms full of warm towels from the dryer. "Mmmmm. Doesn't it smell nice in here?"

"Mom, I am so hairy!" Madison blurted out.

"Did you say *hairy*?" Mom couldn't help but chuckle.

"Yes, hairy. Right here. On my legs." Madison rubbed her calf. "I always knew I had little hairs but I never noticed how much they were growing before now and look! I'm as *furry* as Phin, Mom."

"No you're not!" Mom smiled. "Honey, human beings have hair on their legs and that's just the way it goes. We've talked about shaving before. It's not *disgusting*, it just is. I guess maybe we need to get you a razor."

"Mom, I'm not ready to shave!"

"Okay, girlie, stay hairy then," Mom joked.

Madison was over-thinking again—about razors and shaving and being hairy forever and ever and to infinity. Who else did Madison know who shaved her legs?

Mom did most of the time.

Aimee had also started shaving just last year, but she was blond, so you could barely see the hair anyway.

Madison wondered if Fiona had to shave.

"Okay, okay, give me the razor," Madison decided at last.

Mom pulled out one of her disposable plastic razors and a tube of aloe cream. "I promise it won't hurt, honey bear."

First, Mom demonstrated on herself. Then she shaved a strip on Maddie's leg.

Finally, Madison tried on herself, real slow. She only nicked herself twice, which Mom said was pretty good. Soon enough the leg fuzz was gone and little hairs were dancing on top of the bath water.

"Ewwwch! It stings," Madison said, dunking her legs back in the tub.

"Only for a moment," Mom sighed. "My big girl."

Madison rolled her eyes. "Yeah, Mom, whatever. I'm twelve, remember? You can cut out all that sappy stuff, all right?"

"Well, I'll let you finish up." She kissed the top of Maddie's wet head.

"Yeah, can you go now?" Madison asked. "Like *NOW*."

"Oh!" She pulled something out of her pocket. "I almost forgot. You got a letter yesterday."

Mom dropped an envelope on the counter, winked, and shut the bathroom door.

There on the sinktop was a letter written on deep-sea-blue stationery, Aimee's favorite color. The silver ink on the envelope was already a little smudged from water on the counter, so Madison ripped it open right away. It felt like opening her arms for a giant hug.

Dear Maddie . . .

Oh I miss you soooooo much!!!!! How are you doing at home? I am sorry that I haven't really

written except like twice this summer but I have been dancing every single day and I am sooooooo tired. I actually got on pointe last week, can you BELIEVE it??? The teacher says that the toe shoes will probably make our toes ache and bleed sometimes which is awful, but I want to be a dancer so I better just deal with that.

I miss you! Did I say that already? You would love camp sooooo much, Maddie, I know you would. There are the coolest people here. Of course it is a dance camp of all kinds so there are not just ballet dancers but jazz and tap too. Everyone eats together and we do other stuff like swimming and arts and crafts and have camp nights where we sing songs and tell stories and roast marshmallows and sometimes go on skunk patrol which is this game we play and oh it is the best ever. Did I say I MISS YOU??? I do.

I have made so many new friends too and I just know you would love them. This one girl Sasha is from Russia originally and she lives in New York City. She is so cool and I think we might see each other when I get back. Then there is this other girl Chelsea and she

Aimee had only been gone a month and already she

was making new best friends? Madison kept reading.

is TOTALLY cool, she's 15 and she has a tattoo! Can you believe that?

So the funnest part of the whole camp for me is this one counselor named Josh. OK, he is to die! He is such a total hottie. He teaches modern dance and I think he looks like he should be a movie star or something. Seriously!

Anyway, I decided for the last week of camp I am going to take his lessons as a dance elective and that way I get to see him like every single day. I know that he is like way, way older than me but I don't even care he is so, so cute!!! Can you imagine going out with someone like that? I think about him all the time. Sometimes I wish I was 16 already. I am like in love with him. Is that possible???? Maybe something could happen, you never know.

Well, I just wanted you to know that I miss you and all that. I will be back home a couple of days before school starts and I will call you like the very second I get home. Have you heard from Egg? I miss him too even if he is a total pain in the butt. I am so glad we are finally starting 7th grade. Now I can qualify to be in the Far Hills Junior High Dance Troupe and that is something I have wanted forever.

How are your Mom and Dad and the snuggly puggly?

Okay, I'm going now. I have Josh's class this afternoon and I am so psyched!!! I want to look just right and act just right, right?

Bye!!! I luv you more than ice cream!

Luv, Aimee

P.S. As soon as I get home I will call you I promise!

While Madison couldn't deal with the hives of change, Aimee was in a huge rush to change everything. How could she be crushing on a camp counselor? Madison hadn't even given boys too much thought lately. They all seemed pretty stupid and dorky to her.

"Camp must change the way you think about stuff," Madison mused, and put the letter in her desk for safekeeping. She'd scan it into her Aimee file later.

"Maaaaadison," Mom suddenly screeched from downstairs. "Are you still in the bathroom? Get moving, I need your help."

Mom always needed something. Ever since Dad moved out, Mom needed help cleaning, gardening, organizing, and all that. She needed help so she could get her own film work done. Whenever Mom went away on an overnight business trip she said, "I need your help holding down the fort, honey."

Whenever Mom was going to be gone for more than a few days, she said, "I need your help while I'm gone. I want you be good for the Gillespies," or whomever Madison was staying with during that trip.

The truth was, "help" was Madison's real middle name.

Madison Francesca *Help* Finn.

"In a minute, Mom!" Madison screamed back. Of course, she should have said "In twenty-six minutes, Mom," because that was how long it took Madison to actually get downstairs. But once they started cleaning up, the two of them accomplished a lot. She and Mom washed the kitchen floor and repotted some of Mom's orchids.

After the general house "summer cleaning" was done, Mom raised her eyebrows and in her best Wicked Witch from *The Wizard of Oz* voice, said, "Weeeell, my pretty . . . now it's time to clean your ROOM!"

Officially, she didn't bug Madison about cleaning her bedroom until the laundry factor got out of control. Unfortunately, today was that day. Madison's hamper was overflowing onto the floor and Mom had seen it. Mom had a mantra: Clean up your mess, say bye-bye to stress.

"Madison, my pretty," Mom whined like the Wicked Witch again. "Go pick up your room now before I lock you up in it forever!"

Mom was such a weirdo sometimes. That's where Madison got her weirdness—definitely.

All joking aside, Madison was happy to straighten up the piles of clothes and books and magazine clippings in her bedroom. After an hour or two, she'd even finished a collage card for Aimee.

Inspired by Aimee's letter, she pasted a picture of some cute guy on the front of the card and drew a big arrow with the words *Josh & Aimee 4-Ever*. She even found a clipping of some ballerina that made it look better and more Aimee-like, too.

Madison wondered what Josh *really* looked like. She assumed he must be cute, because the cute boys always liked Aimee best.

Finally, Madison signed the card, "I love you more than chocolate shakes, Maddie." They always signed letters with stuff that way. One day back in fourth grade, when they were on the swing set in Aimee's backyard, they had decided to be best friends forever and to love each other forever more than absolutely anything else. That "anything" included ice cream and chocolate shakes, of course. Once Aimee had even sent Madison a card that said, "I luv you like a sister." That meant a lot.

Later on, Madison went online. She'd cleaned, she'd organized, and now she figured it was a good time to check out bigfishbowl.com again.

On the home page, Madison scanned the list of names currently logged onto bigfishbowl.com. A bigfishbowl.com moderator (also known as Shark) led off the list. (The sites were required to have some Web police person who tried to keep people from cursing or saying nasty things to the other members.) This site prided itself in being super safe. Mom liked that—and so did Madison.

```
Shark
Cuteguy87
Mystake
Wuzupgrl
PC_cake
Bethiscool
Imagoodie
Peacefish
HelPer
Bigwheels
```

Bigwheels?

Madison couldn't believe it. Her "only the lonely" chat buddy was somewhere on the site—right now. That meant Madison could IM her. IM stood for Insta-message. It was like having a live conversation on the computer.

```
<MadFinn>: heybigwheels remember me
   only the
<MadFinn>: lonely?
```

In less than ten seconds, a message back popped up.

<Bigwheels>: Hello!!! Oh WOW its u! 2K4W!! HIG?

<MadFinn>: 2K4W? HIG?

<Bigwheels>: 2 kool 4 words! Howz It Going? LOL

<MadFinn>: ya LOL

<MadFinn>: I thought about what u said B4 about being alone I am alone a lot too

<Bigwheels>: when does your school start????

<MadFinn>: next week and my friend is comin home

<Bigwheels>: I cantbelieve u looked me up sooo KOOL

<MadFinn>: ;>) I WANNA BE KEYPALS OR WHATEVER oops sorry I hit capslock

<Bigwheels>: ok em me it's just bigwheels@email

<MadFinn>: madfinn@email too

<Bigwheels>: hey BRB

<MadFinn>: Hello??

<MadFinn>: Are you AFK?

BRB meant "be right back."

AFK meant "away from keyboard."

Madison had learned a lot of online lingo from Egg.

But Bigwheels stayed away for longer than BRB. She was AFK for at least five minutes! Madison was forced to log off again.

That night, after Mom's takeout sushi supper, Madison returned to her file.

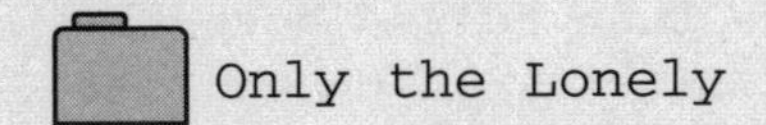

Alone once again. Big surprise. This will be the file that gets filled the fastest, no doubt.

Dad called again. He thinks he might be coming home a lot later than he said in his e-mail and he was checking to make sure we were on for dinner as soon as he got back. He doesn't want me to feel left out but he sure sounded so far away. Then again, everyone feels far away to me these days. I guess Dad's new Internet company start-up is going well, though. He has his fingers in a lot of different pies; that's what Mom always says. He calls himself an entrepreneur (that is a huge word, I had to look it up to spell it!). Maybe Dad can help me find Bigwheels online?

I couldn't believe that Mom and I had sushi tonight. It's a little more interesting than pizza even though I think raw fish is maybe the grossest thing on the entire planet except headcheese and pig's feet, which I saw at the butcher's once. I must admit that I did like the California roll sushi a teeny bit. It was just vegetables and rice and a little bit of seaweed, which wasn't so bad. But forget the tuna roll!!! That wasn't anything like

tuna from the cans (Mom lied) so I spit it right out right away. Not even Phin the animal garbage disposal would eat that!

If I don't like tuna rolls, does that mean I am not an adventurous person? If I'm not an adventurous person, does that mean that I am going to be snubbed in junior high as some kind of loser? If I am branded as a loser, does that mean I'll be alone forever?

For Madison, all over-thoughts led back to one place: the lonely, looming doom of seventh grade. It was less than two weeks away.

Madison wished she could see Fiona again.

She needed a real friend real fast.

They had swapped phone numbers, but who would be the first to call?

Chapter 4

The next day, while Madison was taking a predictable walk around the block, something quite unpredictable happened.

Phin took a sharp corner, got loose, and ran full speed ahead, tongue wagging along with his curlicue tail.

Naturally, he was chasing a C-A-T.

"Stop! Phin!" Madison shouted, almost catching up with him. That's when she saw the car. Phin was on a one-way collision course with—

"STOOOOP! Phiiiiiiiiin!"

Someone in the car must have seen Madison darting down the street like a cartoon character, hands waving in the air. The car screeched to a stop.

Phin stopped too, collapsing at the curb.

"Are you okay? Phinnie?" Madison rushed over. He sputtered and sneezed, stunned by all the activity. He was probably mad that he'd missed the cat, too. Madison wrapped her arms around his furry body and guided him onto the sidewalk. He licked her hand.

The girl who had jumped out of the car rushed over, talking too fast. "Oh, Madison! Is he okay? Oh, my dad didn't see him. He just came out of nowhere—"

Madison looked up. "Fiona?"

"Is your doggy okay?"

"Phin's fine." Madison smiled.

By now Mr. Waters had pulled his car to the side of the street so the rest of the traffic could pass.

"Young lady, you have one lucky dog there," Mr. Waters said, as he also got out of the car. "I turned my head for a moment and—whammo—we almost hit the little guy. You just can't be too careful these days, can you? Hey there, little fella."

Phin wagged his tail, shaking his whole butt. He got excited around strangers. No one could have guessed that Phin just missed crashing into a car. He was loving all this attention.

"Dad, this is Madison. We just met the other day, actually. We're going to be in the same grade at Far Hills this fall."

Madison couldn't believe she was sitting on the

pavement, holding Phin and talking to Fiona and Mr. Waters. Now she *definitely* believed that some kind of cosmic forces were pulling her together with this new girl.

And now no one had to worry about who called whom first.

"Well, Miss Madison," Mr. Waters continued, "how about we give you and that pooch a lift back home? He's shaking like a leaf."

Fiona's Dad helped lift the dog into the back seat of the car.

Madison showed him the way home.

It took thirty seconds.

"What a pretty house," Fiona said as the car tires crunched up the gravel driveway.

"Thanks," Madison shrugged from the backseat.

"It was very nice meeting you, Miss Madison," said Mr. Waters in a very low voice. He sounded like Darth Vader's brother. "And you too, little doggy."

"Rowrooo!" Phin howled back.

Fiona called out cheerily from the car window as they pulled away, "Maybe we can hang out later? I don't really have any—well—it would be fun, do you think?"

"Do I think?" Madison laughed and then quickly added, "*Way* too much. Wanna hang tomorrow maybe?"

"Yeah! Come to my house around twelve," Fiona cried. "You know where I live! Bye!"

As the car made a turn onto the street, Mr. Waters honked his horn good-bye.

Madison hardly ate any dinner that night. Suddenly life had gotten interesting, or at least she hoped so. It was better than TV or bigfishbowl.com, and Phin even deserved some of the credit.

"What a good dog," Madison cooed at him that night when she went to bed. "I am sorry you almost got run over, Phinnie, but thanks to you I get to hang out with Fiona again."

The next day, Madison knocked on her new friend's door around lunchtime. She got there at twelve noon *exactly* because she didn't want to risk being late, early, or in between. It was twelve on the dot.

A boy answered the bell. He was at least a foot taller than Madison.

"Hey!" he grunted. "You here for Fiona?"

Madison guessed he was Fiona's twin brother, Chet, since they looked exactly the same. The only difference was that he had fuzz on his face, and was a lot taller.

Chet was just back from band camp and he was in a bad mood. He yelled upstairs for his sister and then flopped back onto the sofa in front of a giant TV set until Fiona came down the stairs a minute later.

"How was camp?" Madison asked.

"Camp is what it is," Chet said in a monotone.

Madison was certain this conversation was going nowhere. Thankfully, Fiona appeared.

"Madison! I am so glad you came! Do you wanna go for a walk and maybe get an ice-cream cone or something?"

They spent the next hour walking into the old town part of Far Hills, near the train station, past the ice cream Freeze Palace, of course; a discount shoe-repair place; a bakery; Wink's Pet Store; and some other places. Madison gave Fiona a neighborhood tour.

"I go to Wink's when I'm feeling bummed out," Madison admitted. "They have cool tropical fish and actually it's where I got Phin when he was just a baby. He's almost four now."

"I don't have any pets," said Fiona. "I'm so jealous of you. Phin is a total cutie. I love those snorty noses."

It was the beginning of a great week.

On the second day, Madison and Fiona went to Freeze Palace for two scoops of Raspberry Bliss, a new homemade flavor.

On the third day, they skipped the cones and bought an entire pint of Cherry Garcia at the store and sat on the Waterses' porch to eat it spoonful by yummy spoonful right out of the container. These days, for Madison and Fiona, life was just a bowl of Cherry Garcia.

Of course, day three wasn't all cherry ice cream.

That was the day when Madison saw a *very* different side of Chet Waters. He threw a fit at his sister. "You're such a mega-loser, Fi-moan-a!" he screeched. Madison thought at first he was a major crybaby, but then she realized that maybe he was just jealous because his sister had a new friend and he didn't. Maybe he was only the lonely, too?

Fiona was not as sympathetic. "My brother Chet is not lonely—he's just a load. Ever since he got home from camp, all he can do is play Age of Empires and pick on me. He won't even let me online when he's home."

"You go online?" asked Madison.

"Of course! I totally love computers. I gave you my e-mail, right?"

Madison made a mental note: send Fiona an e-mail soon. She didn't want Fiona to think she'd lost her address.

On the fourth day, Madison and Fiona went clog shopping, because clogs were comfortable and Madison loved them.

On the fifth day, they sat on Fiona's porch and made friendship bracelets from string.

On the sixth day, they went for a long bike ride and Madison met Fiona's mother.

Mrs. Waters kept insisting how thrilled Madison must be to be starting those junior high school years.

"Aren't you just overjoyed?" Mrs. Waters gushed.

Madison didn't really know how to answer that one.

On the one hand, of course she was excited about leaving middle school and starting a whole new life adventure with new friends and new teachers and new after-school activities. On the other hand, she was "run for the hills and don't look back" *terrified*. She was afraid of getting lost on the first day of school. She was afraid of getting swallowed up by all the popular people and trapped in study hall with all the geeks.

Time was flying and suddenly she had this strange feeling like she didn't want the summer to end. Had Fiona changed everything?

"Overjoyed." Madison finally answered Mrs. Waters with middle-of-the-road enthusiasm. "I guess."

And on the seventh and final day of the week, Madison Finn and Fiona Waters had their best afternoon ever together. That was the day when Madison spent the entire day hanging out in Fiona's bedroom. She'd seen it before, of course, but not for such a long time. Madison was learning a few of Fiona's secrets.

Fiona was a collector, too. Madison noticed that right away. Up on a top shelf in Fiona's room, Madison saw a far-out, enormous collection of Beanies.

"I'm really over them," Fiona had to admit, even

though they were dripping off the shelves. "Except for Halo and maybe Mooch, I don't like any of them anymore. I guess I'll just put them in the attic or something."

"You must have like a thousand animals here," Madison said.

"One hundred and fourteen, and they all have tag protectors, too." Fiona said. "They're pretty stupid, though, right? Mom said we should sell them on eBay, but I don't wanna do that yet."

Elsewhere in her room, Fiona had tacked up all sorts of postcards and pictures on a piece of flowered fabric that hung over her bed. Madison leaned in to read some of the cartoons. She pointed to one photo in the center. It showed Fiona and a redheaded girl. They were standing by the ocean.

"What beach is this?" Madison asked. "Who is that?"

"Pacific Ocean, Debbie," Fiona said. She sounded a little sad.

Debbie was Fiona's best friend from where the Waters family used to live in Los Gatos, California. Unfortunately, Fiona's parents only let her call Debbie on weekends, because it was too expensive to talk at other times.

Fiona knew all about Aimee being at ballet camp, too. Madison told her about Egg at computer camp; about Mom and Dad's divorce; about hating chunky peanut butter; and about loving romantic

movies on cable. So far *Love Story* was the top flick on Madison's list. It was an old movie from the '70s that was really romantic *and* really sad. After all, if something made you cry, that meant it was meaningful.

Fiona agreed. In fact, Madison and Fiona seemed to agree on most things.

"Don't you hate it when you miss someone and then you get, like, so bored? Do you know what I mean?"

Madison knew *exactly* what Fiona meant.

"And Mom tells me to just get over it and she and Dad don't understand *anything*," Madison added. "They forgot what it's like to be twelve—"

"Almost thirteen!" Fiona laughed.

They were practically finishing each other's sentences.

On the walk home from Fiona's, Madison's mind buzzed a mile a minute: new friends, new school, new EVERYTHING.

Madison powered up her laptop as soon as she got home.

Can new friends swoop in and take the place of old friends? I don't miss Aimee and Egg as much as I did a week ago. I don't even miss Dad that much, even though it's been a month since I saw him.

Okay, I miss Dad but only a little bit and only because you're supposed to miss your parents, right?

I'm happier than happy about almost every little thing this week, even walking Phinnie, and that is just plain BIZARRO. I haven't even been back into these files in almost

As she thought about what to type in next, Madison realized a very important thing. Her mailbox was blinking.

She hadn't even been back into these files in almost *three* days.

Madison had ten e-mails, but of course eight of them were stupid spam or ads or unimportant chain letters. But she had two real e-mails.

The first one was from her new keypal. She was beginning to think Bigwheels and MadFinn would really stay K4E (Keypals 4 Ever).

From: Bigwheels
To: MadFinn
Subject: I'M ALIVE ARE U?
Date: Sunday 27 Aug 4:42 PM

I hope you aren't MAD! My uncle finally got me a stupid modem that works right. That is why I kept getting disconnected for the last week so I O U an apology. I really did like meeting you in the

bigfishbowl. Maybe we can be keypals after all?

BTW I'm in 7th grade now too. We started already though because I think schools start earlier out west and down south or something like that.

Write back soon or else!
Yours till the butter flies,
Bigwheels

The second one was from her old school pal.

From: Eggaway
To: MadFinn
Subject: hi
Date: Wed 30 Aug 10:01 AM

Hey Madison, where r u? I am now at my gramp's lake house. I am totaly bored. Did you see that new movie Tidal Wave? Say hi to your Mom and dad. See u SOON! I'm leaving tomroow then back in Far Hills on Friday.
p.s. oh yeah does Aim have a bf at camp? She wrote me this queer lettr about some dude. Wuzup?
p.p.s. don't wrtie back i will see you SOON
p.p.p.s. Drew says hi.

Madison was happier than happy that she'd finally heard from her online chat buddy *and* that Egg was on his way home Friday.

Now Aimee would be back on Sunday and then the three of them would be together again and then school would be starting and they'd be best friends all over again just like last year.

Madison opened a file.

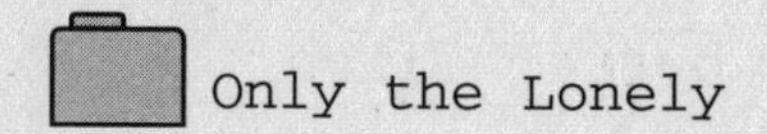

Just when you think change is like the worst thing ever, it turns into a good thing all of a sudden.

Mom and I are getting along good for a change (considering the fact that we argued through most of sixth grade).

Even Daddy is coming home soon. Well, not to *this* home exactly, but he's coming back to his loft in downtown Far Hills.

The stupid cliché is so true. There are gold linings in almost every cloud. Or silver linings, whatever. I just know that things are good at this very moment.

I'm not totally alone anymore.

Madison read the words on her screen. For the first time all summer she was happier than happy.

Chapter 5

Madison looked at the *Simpsons* calendar Mom had stuck up on the fridge. Exactly four days from today junior high was starting. Madison had drawn a giant red circle around the date: September 5.

Madison dialed Fiona's number, but hung up right away. She decided it was Fiona's turn to call her instead. She didn't want to appear like a clingy friend, after all.

Now that Madison was going to be a seventh grader, things like when-to-call etiquette had taken on greater importance. Aimee had always been the one who paid attention to stuff like that, but Madison was trying to figure it out on her own now.

Distractedly, Madison flipped through a copy of a

teen magazine Mom had picked up at the supermarket checkout, staring at the pictures of girls in mini-skirts and super-high platform shoes. How did they stand in those for more than five seconds? How did they bend over?

All the models were wearing glitter makeup and gobs of lip gloss. Madison thought about wearing lip gloss on her lips. Strawberry-Kiwi Smooch was the best flavor and it tasted like candy when you chewed it off. Madison liked Root Beer flavor, too, of course, but that was harder to find.

She wondered if boys liked the way lip gloss tasted when they kissed a girl. Did lip gloss flavor taste different if you chewed if off someone else's lips? Madison had never kissed anyone, so she didn't know from personal experience.

Who else wore lip gloss? Aimee didn't. She hated makeup of all kinds. (Her family, including all four older brothers and their basset hound Blossom, were into granola and all-natural *everything*.)

Did Fiona wear lip gloss? Madison couldn't remember. Had Fiona ever *kissed* someone (besides her parents, of course)? Madison would have to ask her about that.

A few pages after the platforms and lip gloss spread, Madison randomly opened up to a quiz titled "Are You Friends to the End?" She grabbed her favorite orange pen, the one with a Florida navel orange–shaped eraser on top.

1. You have a big algebra test and you haven't even cracked open a book! The night before the test you call your best friends and ask them:
   a) If you can sit nearby and cheat off their test the next day!
   b) To come right over and help you cram for the exam!
   c) If they will help you make up an excuse so you don't have to take the test!

Madison couldn't imagine who would ever pick a) or admit to picking a). She didn't cheat. In fact the entire quiz seemed stupid and obvious. It wasn't exactly the kind of "are you friends?" quiz Madison had hoped for. She was looking for some concrete advice. She also wouldn't make excuses as c) suggested, so Madison selected b).

2. Your mom grounds you and you're stuck at home on the night of the coolest party of the year. You:
   a) Call your friend and beg her to blow off the party and stay with you instead.
   b) Call your friend and wish her a good time at the party! You can't wait to hear all the details!
   c) Call your friend and cry into the phone. Your friend will listen to anything.

Madison selected b) again. She could tell already how this quiz was turning out. She was a "b)" type, which probably meant something like: honest, caring, straightforward, and all that. Sometimes (like right in the middle of this quiz) Madison turned into the "nice" friend. She was sick of that. Sometimes she wanted to be "wild" or "spontaneous" or even a little outrageous. She knew she *must* have those qualities in her somewhere, even though she was the person who always got too embarrassed to even *speak* and usually ran as far away as possible when confronted with any kind of conflict whatsoever.

"Maybe seventh grade will be when I finally take a few more chances," she said hopefully, moving to the next question.

3. Your best friend is away at camp, and you're so bored! Then you meet a new friend in your neighborhood and you start hanging out. Do you:

Madison reread the question *slowly*. What were her choices?

a) Kick your best friend to the curb!
There's a new friend in town!
b) Tell the new friend that you like her
but you already have a "best" friend.
c) Try to see if the two friends might like
each other so you can be a trio instead
of two against one.

Madison started to over-think *every* answer. This was a question pulled from the pages of her life.

What really would happen when Aimee did get back? What would happen once school started? What if Fiona and Aimee hated each other?

Answer a) was definitely out. Madison didn't have a mean bone in her body, and she wouldn't kick anyone to any curb.

Was c) was the right response? Madison wasn't sure.

She played it safe and circled b). After all, she told herself, she and Aimee had been best friends forever and *that* was that. You can have a lot of different friends but you only have one really, truly, madly, deeply, true-blue friend. That was Aimee Anne Gillespie, not Fiona Waters. Not yet.

Madison's head hurt from thinking so much, so she went online to check her e-mail again. This e-mail checking was addictive!

Today the list was longer than usual but it wasn't all friends. dELiA's clothing was having a sale on platform shoes Madison would never, ever wear. Some Joke-A-Day service addressed their message to Attn: Mr. Madison Funn. She deleted them both.

Madison decided to send a few e-mails instead of just sitting around waiting for everyone to write her. She dashed off a note to Dad and sent Egg an e-mail asking how camp was just to annoy him (because of course, camp was O-V-E-R). Finally, she started a note

back to Bigwheels. She hadn't written her terrific bigfishbowl.com friend an "official" e-mail yet. Bigwheels seemed pretty hip. Maybe she had some friendly advice to share?

From: MadFinn
To: Bigwheels
Subject: me with a question
Date: Fri 1 Sept 10:41 AM

Hello? I hope this is the right e-mail address. Thanks for your message the other day. I think this whole keypals thing is a good thing.

Okay so I'm having a not-so-great day so maybe you can cheer me up? I hope so.

The funniest thing about keypals is that for some reason I feel like I could tell you anything. Do you feel that? You really have to know me to know how incredible that is because I am the kind of person who turns beet red and can't form complete sentences when I'm embarrassed. But the jitters go away on e-mail. Like now. Okay, so what else do I wanna say?

What is school like 4 u Washington? Why do they start so early there?

If you can believe it I have no idea what my school is even like b/c I have only seen it from the outside. I told you it's Junior High. How do you stop yourself from being so nervous about all the new school things? Do you do something? Do you have any pets? Do you have any brothers or sisters? Do you believe in God?

I guess I have a lot of questions. You don't have to answer any of these, of course, but it would be cool if you did. I guess if we're going to be keypals we should be honest with each other.

Yours till the chocolate chips,
MadFinn

p.s. write back or else!!!

As Madison finished her e-mail, an IM box popped up on her screen.

Insta-message to Madfinn
<<Emily114>>: Wanna talk?

Madison didn't recognize the screen name. It was some random person online. Both her Mom and Dad told her never to respond to people she didn't know. Madison deleted the dialogue box and then clicked offline.

Right after she closed down her computer, the phone rang. Madison nearly jumped out of her skin. Madison did the phone call math inside her head. This call was definitely from Fiona.

She had *said* she would call, after all.

"Got it, Mom!" Madison yelled, catching it on the fourth ring, gasping into the receiver, "Hello?"

"Ma-di-son?" a boy's voice taunted.

That wasn't Fiona. That was . . .

"Egg!" Madison exclaimed, happy to hear his voice but unable to totally mask her disappointment. She'd been crossing her fingers for Fiona.

"Whassup!?! I am back as of like twenty minutes ago thanks to my dad busting the speed limit all the way from Vermont and we are so hanging out today! Yes we are, you and me and—"

"Egg?" Madison tried to get a word in. "Why don't—"

"Hey, hey, hey! Maddie, you didn't say anything about my e-mails! Did you get my e-mails? I have so much to tell you and I have the coolest new thing to show you and—"

"Egg? Why don't you just come over!" Madison barked.

"Okay," Egg barked back.

She threw herself across the living room sofa. From where she was draped, she could see the kitchen stove's digital clock readout: 11:11. She made a wish on the numbers. (When four ones lined up like that, your wish was supposed to come true, or at least that's what Egg's older sister Mariah always said.) Madison wished Fiona would just call already.

"Hey, Mom, did anyone call this morning?" Madison cried out.

"The phone just rang, dear, didn't you pick it up?"

"No, like maybe when I was asleep late and you just forgot to tell me?"

"No, honey. No one called. Check the caller ID."

Now the clock said 11:14. Madison had spent the entire morning playing the waiting game.

The doorbell rang and Madison jumped.

How would she greet Egg? A smack on the *head*? He deserved it! She opened the door, laughing.

"Fiona?"

Fiona rocked from foot to foot, hands in her cargo pants pockets. Madison could see Mr. and Mrs. Waters and even Chet waiting out in the car so she quickly used the door as a shield. She didn't feel like waving or smiling or dealing with parents in any way right now.

"Oh, Madison, I'm sorry to just show up like this,"

Fiona said. "I forgot to tell you about my mom taking me and Chet over to the mall again today to get some more clothes for school. I told her you and I said we'd hang out today since I've never been over to your house, but I really have to go shopping again because she said so."

"Okay," Madison said, a little numb from the surprise.

"But you can come along too, if you want. She said that was okay too. Do you wanna?"

Madison looked at her feet. "Fiona, I look awful in my sweats."

"That's okay. We can wait for you to change. Come on . . ."

"W-w-well . . ."

"It'll be so much fun," Fiona blurted again, "even if my pain-in-the-butt brother does have to come along."

"W-w-well . . ." Madison said again, "the truth is that I can't."

"Oh," Fiona seemed genuinely disappointed. "Oh, well. Are you sure?"

"It's just that one of my friends, Egg, is back from camp and he's coming over like right now and—I can't. Look, I'm really sorry."

"Oh, well, I'll call you later, maybe?"

"That would be cool. Let's talk later."

"You're sure you can't come?"

"Sorry." Madison shook her head.

"Okay, I'll call you!" Fiona bounced down the stairs and across Madison's lawn into her family's car. She actually looked like she was running away. Of course Madison knew she wasn't running away. *Madison* was the only one who ran away from things.

"'Bye!" Madison cried out after her, a little too late.

Mr. Waters honked the horn good-bye. The car pulled away. Madison walked back inside and flopped back onto the sofa.

"Is Fiona mad at me?" she wondered aloud.

Phin just snored.

She suddenly felt very alone again.

Chapter 6

"Surprise!"

Egg screeched and made a ridiculous piggy face at Madison. He did this gross thing where he pushed his nose up so his nostrils looked like pig nostrils and then he made this awful sucking noise against his top teeth.

"I'm baaaaaack!" he yelped.

Madison couldn't help but giggle. "Egg! You doof! You freaked me out."

Egg smacked her shoulder with a loud *Slap!* "You're a doof, DOOF!"

He bounded inside and quickly whipped off his backpack.

"Maddie there is the coolest thing ever invented

I have to show you right now! Look at this—"

Mom walked into the living room at that exact moment.

"Well, Walter! Welcome home! You look like you had a good time at camp. You also look taller."

Egg was panting like Phin at this point, hot from the summer heat. Madison noticed that he was taller and had even more freckles than usual.

"Yeah, Mrs. Finn," Egg said. "Grew two and a half inches. Lost four pounds. Camp was okay. At least I didn't get picked on or anything. It was a whole bunch of us computer-heads. What's up with you?"

"You are such a major computer EGG-head, Egg!" Madison laughed.

"Am not!" he snapped back.

"Are too!" she retorted.

"Am not!" he snapped back again.

"Well, it's nice to see you again, Walter. Don't get into any trouble. No fighting." Madison's Mom cautioned with a big grin. "I mean it."

"Mom, why would we get into a fight? I haven't seen Egg in forever!"

Egg hurriedly unzipped his backpack. Phin was sniffing around the varnished wood floor where he'd put it down.

"Is that some kind of calculator?" Madison asked when he pulled out his latest toy.

"No, no, it's not a calculator, it's like this miniature computer. Here, look, look at how cool this is."

He showed it to Madison, who oohed and aahed.

"This is way cool," she said.

Egg patted Phin's head a little too hard. "Yeah, yeah, get lost, doggy."

"Hey! Don't talk to Phinnie that way! Come here, Phin."

Egg teased, "He is still fat! Ha-ha-ha! Ugly pugly!"

"Cut it out." Madison bonked the top of Egg's head. Then she punched a few buttons on his computer. "This really is very cool, *Walter*."

Madison was glad to have Egg back home, even if he teased her. She could, after all, tease him right back. That's what friends were for.

He showed Madison how he'd downloaded an entire copy of some kids' science encyclopedia off the Internet.

"Why would you do that?" she asked.

"Uh, I dunno. Because I could?"

Madison wanted to tell Egg about her new computer, too, but at that moment Mom walked back into the room with a tray of toasted blueberry Pop-Tarts and Egg's eyes got as big as saucers.

Egg was easily distracted by TV, computers, and *any* kind of food.

"Pop-Tarts! Mrs. Finn, you are like the best cook ever!" Egg exclaimed.

Madison couldn't believe anyone would call her mother the best cook ever.

Egg had eaten two tarts before he noticed what time it was. "It's 11:34! Hey Maddie, you still have cable? Wrestling is on now! I missed WWF so much when I was at camp. Madison, can we put it on?"

This was predictable too: Egg wanted to watch wrestling every time he came over. The Diaz family didn't believe in cable television. They stuck to broadcast channels only. They had barely even managed to put an antenna on the roof.

So Madison flicked on the tube. Egg beamed.

"I'm going upstairs to change, okay?" Madison said.

"Huh? Yeah. Okay." Egg's eyes were fixed on the screen.

A whole summer had gone by, and Egg was still a wrestling freak! Madison thought shows like *RAW* were so dumb, but she couldn't exactly tell Egg that. What was the point to wrestling? It was so fake. She pulled on a pair of shorts and an orange halter top and went back downstairs.

Egg was *still* in a TV coma. Madison seriously began to question her motives in ditching Fiona and keeping the plans with Egg.

"The Rock is so cool! Stone Cold Steve—WOW! Look at them. This is AWESOME," Egg cried out, engrossed by the action. "Check that OUT, Madison!"

Madison squirmed into her seat. She and Egg hadn't seen each other in over a month, and

already things were back to the way they had been before. *Why* was that? They were doing that hanging-out-but-not-really-hanging-out thing that they'd been doing since Miss Jeremiah's kindergarten class.

Spending an afternoon with Egg almost always meant doing what Egg wanted. Boy stuff.

Madison picked up Phin and put him onto her lap. "Good dog," she cooed into his ear. It twitched. Pugs have sensitive ears.

"Look at that! Look at that!" Egg shrieked. He was shouting nonstop, sitting on the edge of Madison's sofa, eyes glazed over. "Go, go, slam him! Awwww!"

Phin jumped off Madison's lap and scurried into the other room. Even Phin didn't want to put up with *this*.

Madison had one of her over-thoughts.

Here she was, having spent the past few days believing she'd developed an allergy to change, believing that her entire universe was in a state of constant flux, but right here and now she realized that she was experiencing a hundred-percent "allergy-free" moment.

I guess there really are some things that never change, Madison thought.

Here she was, sitting in her living room with one of her oldest, best-est pals, watching the same show as always, saying the same things she and he always

said, eating the same snack foods she and he always ate. Even Phin was bored; he'd already left the room.

"Hey, Egg, do you mind if I go up to my room for a minute?" Madison interrupted his wrestling show.

"What? Yeah. Sure." Egg was so distracted.

"Just come up when it's over." Madison said and walked upstairs. It was better this way.

Egg

Wrestling is the stupidest thing on the planet and I am so glad that Fiona is not a wrestling fan. At least, there were no wrestling posters hanging in her room anywhere. I wonder if Chet is a wrestling fan?

Rude Awakening: Be careful what you wish for. I wished for Egg and now I'm just not sure I feel like hanging around to do *this*. I don't feel like watching *RAW*, Egg! Ha ha. Very funny.

Why is it when people go away for the summer that you remember friends differently than they really and truly are? Like Egg, for example. Why are things always better when

"You got a new computer!" Egg sneaked up behind Madison. "How much memory you got?"

"I remember plenty of things," she quipped.

"Ha, ha—very funny," Egg made a face and sat down next to her.

"Hey!" she covered up the computer. "Egg, this is private."

Egg made a face. "I don't care what you're doing. Come on and just close your stupid files. Let's go online and play a game. I hear there are downloadable versions of some great arcade games like Space Invaders or Frogger. You'll love it. Those are so easy."

"But I'm in the middle of something, Egg."

"Come on, wrestling's over. I'm bored. Let's go online. Hey, I know this awesome gaming site. Let's go," he said, leaning over to type in the Web address. "We could play *Who Wants to be a Millionaire* or they also have this wrestling game that is so cool."

"Wrestling? I don't think so."

"Please?" Egg begged.

"No way."

"Oh, Madison, pretty please with sugar and cherries and a bucket of whipped cream on top . . . please?"

"Oh, whatever," Madison sighed, half smiling at his pathetic gestures. "What's the Web address?"

He'd only been over for an hour, and already Madison wondered what it was that she had missed about Egg.

He was rude and he was obsessed with stupid wrestling! A game site with a *wrestling* game? Madison rolled her eyes.

Egg found the site. "Yeah! Okay, I'm gonna be The Undertaker. Who do you want to be? Lemme just download this and enter my password. . . ."

Egg wanted to be The Undertaker.

Madison wanted to be . . . *anywhere but here!*

She used to think Egg's computer games were fun. Now, they seemed so stupid.

"Egg, are you ready to start seventh grade?" Madison asked while he was punching away at the keyboard.

"Wha?" He was too busy getting ready to rumble. "What did you say?"

What had happened to the Egg who played night tag until the mosquitoes got too hungry and the streets got too dark? Where was the Egg who dressed up as a kangaroo three years in a row for Halloween and who thought wrestling was too *violent*?

"Get ready to . . . RUMMMBLE!" Egg was laughing hysterically at the announcer's voice and the mayhem on the computer. He'd also turned up the volume so Madison had to talk louder in order to be heard a little bit.

"Egg! I asked what you were thinking about starting at Far Hills. Have you thought about junior high?"

"YES!" he screeched without even flinching. Madison could not tell if he was answering her question or smacking some other wrestler down with a metal folding chair.

Madison crossed her arms. "Egg, did I tell you

that I'm blasting off for Mars and that planet Earth is about to explode and that little aliens are coming to take you apart piece by piece . . . ?

"YES!" he screeched again.

Egg was hopeless.

But thankfully, after a few more rounds of Smack Down! and one more Pop-Tart (for the road), Egg left. As happy as she had been to see him, Madison was even happier to see him leave, at least for now.

She made a note to say "NO WAY" next time he asked to watch wrestling.

After Egg had left, Madison called Fiona's house, but no one was there. The machine picked up.

"Hey, Fiona, it's Maddie and I'm sorry about today. I wasn't sure if—well, call me and we can talk. I just wanted to make sure you were—"

Beeeeeeeep.

The machine clicked off.

Madison opened her computer.

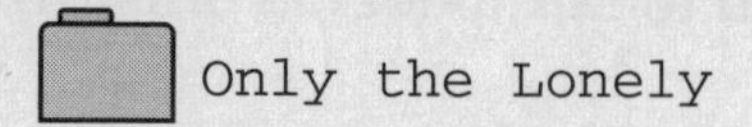

I think everyone in my life took an annoying pill. For whatever reason, Egg is just the most annoying boy I have ever met in my entire life. Okay, maybe he's not different at all, maybe he just is exactly the same and I just forgot how ANNOYING he was! What's the deal with the wrestling anyhow?

Walter Egg Diaz is a BIG GEEK. And I feel bad even thinking (let alone writing that down) because I don't want to be the kind of person who puts people into boxes and judges them for stupid stuff like what they wear or who they hang with or what they watch on televison like WRESTLING. I don't *want* to but somehow I always end up doing just that.

I guess when it comes right down to it, people could stereotype me, too. I mean I am a little bit of a computer geek myself. But the truth is I am NOT the Nutty Professor or some kind of genius or anything with a label on it. I am just Madison Francesca Finn who happens to like computers and happens to like science and math and who happens to be good at remembering things. I like animals, too but that doesn't mean I want to live in a zoo.

Am I being unfair? I know. Egg just happens to be a regular guy who happens to like computers and (groan) wrestling. And I need to stop being so harsh. He's my best *guy* friend.

Sometimes when everything around me is changing, it feels like the world is so different and I wonder when and how did this all happen to me? Why did everyone go and change like this?

Then I realize that it's really not Egg or Aimee or Mom or Dad or even Phin that is doing all the changing.

It's just *me*.

Chapter 7

"Yo, who's this?" Chet was the one growling into the phone.

"Is Fiona there?" Madison asked. "Uh, is this Chet? Is your sister there? This is Madison."

She heard him grunt another "yo," and then scream for his sister, who picked up a second phone.

"Madison?" Fiona chirped.

"Hey, Fiona, I called to say hi. And . . . well, I thought you were going to call me back yesterday. I left a message—"

"Oh really?" Fiona paused. "I did? You did?"

Fiona was a little spacey, which bugged Madison more than she thought. How could she have *forgotten*?

Fiona glossed right over any questions Madison was asking. She was on to the next thing already.

"Hey, Madison, wanna hang today? Mom and Dad have to go do something in the city and I would do anything to get away from evil Chet and his stupid new friends—they are so GROSS. Can I come over to your house for a change?"

Madison invited her over. For some reason, Fiona hadn't hung out at the Finns' yet.

When she arrived, Fiona was wearing another cool outfit, just as nice as the pretty yellow sundress from the mall. She had on a flowered top and capri pants, and her braids were pulled back with a purple ribbon.

"Rowrroooo!" Phin greeted her at the door, his tail wagging a mile a minute. Madison saw this as the best sign yet that in spite of her spacey self, Fiona was a BFTB (best-friend-to-be). Phin was an excellent judge of character.

"Why did you ask me to bring a picture of myself?" Fiona blurted as soon as she entered Madison Finn's front hallway.

"I can't tell you yet," Madison answered. "FIRST . . . I made us smoothies. Hungry?"

"I'm always starving," Fiona said as she took a huge slurp of shake. She spit it out right away. "Is this banana?"

Madison nodded. She had blended together vanilla yogurt with frozen bananas. It was her favorite recipe.

"Oh, bananas make me puke," Fiona said, sticking her tongue out and looking for a glass of water. "Sorry. I'm not really into fruit."

Madison apologized and made a plain vanilla smoothie. She made a mental note, too, for the Fiona file: no fruit—EVER.

"Wow, you have such a nice place, can I see your room?" Fiona asked.

Madison took her upstairs.

"Is that *her*?" Fiona pointed to a photo of Aimee tacked to Madison's door. "That's Annie, right?"

"Annie who?" Madison looked. "You mean Aimee?"

"Your friend, the one who's at camp?" Fiona queried again. "She looks so nice. Is she nice? Duh. Of course she's nice—she's your friend. That was a stupid question."

Madison nodded, but it didn't really matter. She noticed how sometimes Fiona started and finished a conversation all by herself.

"Who's *that*?" Fiona asked, pointing to a second photo with Egg in it.

"Oh, that's Egg—well his real name is Walter. Walter Diaz. He'll go to Far Hills too. He's a nice guy even if he does like wrestling more than life itself sometimes. Well, you'll probably meet him soon."

"Yeah," Fiona snickered. "He's pretty cute, isn't he?"

Madison stopped the tour. Had Fiona actually used the words *Egg* and *cute* in the same sentence?

"Fiona, did you just say Egg was *cute*?"

"He is, Madison. He's like totally my type. You said his name was Walter?" Fiona was actually *staring* at his picture.

In that brief moment, Madison realized that she had SO much to learn about Fiona if they were going to be friends. She had to learn about bananas and other foods that made Fiona puke. She had to learn when Fiona was being a space case and when she was really ignoring Madison. She even had to learn that sometimes Fiona might just see someone like Egg as a cutie. Being a friend with someone new suddenly meant learning lots of new stuff.

From the moment Madison had said "Make yourself at home" inside her room, Fiona had started snooping around like a kid in a toy shop. First she picked up Madison's stuffed Beary, an oversized Teddy Bear with bald patches from where he'd been loved a little too much.

"Is his eye missing?" Fiona asked.

Madison grinned. "I chewed it off when I was two, I think."

Fiona examined Madison's glitter nail polish, picked over a basket of junk on her dresser, and read every CD case and book spine on the bookshelf. Meanwhile, Madison just stood by and let herself be *inspected*. She had been nervous about sharing her house and her stuff, but now Madison wanted Fiona to know everything.

"Oh, do you like Calvin and Hobbes too?"

Madison nodded.

"Is orange your favorite color or what?"

Madison grinned.

"Who's this guy? Is he your boyfriend or something?"

Madison grimaced. "NO WAY!"

Fiona was looking at a framed photograph of Madison with Hart Jones, a gross-out geek from her class. It had been taken on a second-grade field trip to Lake Wannalotta upstate. The only reason Madison had it on her shelf was because she and Hart were holding up this humongous sunfish between them. It was funny, so she'd kept it. Now she realized she'd better replace it. She didn't want people to get the wrong idea, especially people like Fiona.

"Lucky thing this Hart guy left at the end of second grade. He was like a walking zombie, always tagging along with me and Aimee and Egg, and pestering me. Ugh. His family moved." Madison said quickly.

"Hey, what's *this*?" Fiona asked when she saw a framed collage over Madison's bed.

Madison explained that she liked cutting out words and images from magazines and pasting them all together to make a picture. The collage hanging over her bed was themed around the subject of "family." She'd glued pictures of babies next to

words like *Need You* and *Comfort.* There was a border of lace around the edges.

"You are a wicked good artist, Madison," Fiona smiled when she said that. "I mean it. You should take art in school. Have you ever? I can't draw to save my life. I'm so jealous!"

"Gee, thanks." Madison shrugged again. She figured Fiona was just trying to be nice since they were only starting out as friends. "I don't really consider myself to be any kind of real artist, but I like it. I mean it's not *drawing*, exactly . . ."

"Maybe we should take an art elective or something *together* this year?" Fiona suggested. "You can help me with art!"

"What are your hobbies, Fiona?" Madison asked.

"Hmmm. I know I'm gonna try out for soccer this year. Does sports count as a hobby? Chet plays basketball and everyone usually tries to get me to do that too because I'm tall, but I think I'm going for seventh-grade soccer."

"You're into sports?" Madison plopped down on her bed.

Fiona smirked, "Oh yeah, I am *totally* into sports. Big time." She sat down next to Madison.

They decided to sign up for art class *and* try out for soccer together when school started the following week. Maybe soccer could help Madison get rid of her klutziness? She hoped so.

Madison clicked her computer on. She wanted to

show Fiona her computer and all the stuff it could do, including a special program Mom had given her. This software called *Makeover Magic* could morph Madison's—and anyone else's—face into a whole new look.

"Now . . . *this* is why I wanted you to bring a photo," Madison admitted, "so we can make us both over. I have a photo of me, too. Wanna try?"

Fiona and Madison loaded the program. Once their photos were scanned, they started to play.

First, they tested a blond wig on Fiona's head. She looked like a cross between Brandy and Christina Aguilera.

"I look like a clown!" she cried. "Can you imagine if I dyed my hair blond for real? My parents would KILL ME!"

Madison gave herself brown eyes and a crew cut. "Ha! Look at me! I look like my brother—if I had one!"

They laughed. Fiona tried the full-figure makeover with a whole new style. She put herself into a teeny-tiny, itsy-weenie polka-dot bikini.

"I look like an even bigger fool with this look!" she shrieked. "Would you ever wear something like this in public? I don't think so!"

They both tried to cut and paste on the same exact blondie wig, dress, and shades. They looked like *Charlie's Angels* rejects.

"What else do you have on your computer?" Fiona asked.

"Lots of things," Madison said, feeling a little protective of her files. She really wanted to show off all her stuff to Fiona but decided at the last minute that it was much better *NOT* to share files.

Madison decided there was no harm in *describing* the files though.

"The thing is, I started out keeping real files of pictures of clothes, sunglasses, cool shoes, temporary tattoos and stuff like that, like from all the teen magazines." Madison showed Fiona the stacks of colored folders. "I cut stuff out and keep it in folders and I organize it all by categories so if I need to make something like a card I know where to look and find it."

"You are so organized." Fiona gasped.

"I guess so," Madison tilted her head to the side. "I like to make stuff. Actually, I LOVE to make stuff. And I really like being organized."

"Can I see what's on the computer?" Fiona asked.

Madison shrugged. She suddenly felt *very* protective of her online files. But Fiona didn't ask again. She just kept talking.

"I need to get organized in a BIG way," Fiona continued. "I still have all these boxes to unpack from our California move! Plus, my Mom and dad expect me to be like a straight-A student in junior high. They have me like on the advanced placement list at Harvard University already."

"What?" Madison was shocked. "College?"

"Well, not really of course," Fiona said. "But my

dad is like this super achiever and I think he expects us to be the same way. Since Chet is such a lump, I guess that leaves me. I have to do well."

Madison couldn't believe Fiona had even given a single thought to college. It was five years away! But she admired the fact that Fiona wanted to do well in school.

"Hey, Madison, you should store our makeover picture in a new and improved Fashion File," Fiona joked, hitting a few computer keys. "Why am I worried about Harvard for? We can be maw-dells!"

"You really could be a model, you know," Madison said earnestly.

Fiona laughed so hard, she spit. "NOT!"

Madison decided to save the picture of them as "blondie twins" as a screen saver. She'd e-mail it to Fiona, too.

Fiona walked back over to the photo of Egg. "You know, Madison, I really, really, really would love to meet your friend."

"Egg?" Madison gawked. "You may change your mind when you see him up close, Fiona. He's like a real wrestling freak and—"

"I like sports!" Fiona squealed.

Madison laughed.

"Can I ask you a question?"

Fiona shrugged.

"Hey, have you ever kissed a boy?"

Fiona smiled coyly. "Sure. Twice. Two different boys."

"Two? You have to tell me about it."

"Well." Fiona thought for a minute. "There was this guy I was in love with in California and we were boyfriend and girlfriend for a year. We really were in love, I swear. His name was Julio and we saw each other at the beach for this school volleyball squad and then we saw each other every single Thursday for a year. In the beginning we were just like smiling at each other. But this one time after a scrimmage, I got a point in and he grabbed me and kissed me, right there in front of everyone."

"Were you embarrassed? I would have been so embarrassed!"

"A little bit. I was more embarrassed by the fact that everyone started clapping and hooting. But whatever. I was secretly hoping he would do it again. It wasn't a long kiss, the first one, but it was just so nice."

"Did he kiss you again?"

Fiona dropped her head. "Yeah. A lot."

"So what happened?"

Fiona frowned. "He kissed my friend Claire, too. A lot."

"Uh-oh." Madison made a face. "What about the other guy?"

"Okay, that guy was just a dare. Maybe it doesn't count exactly, but it was a dare and I kissed this eighth grader, Clark Cook, on the last day of school last year. He wasn't even that cute. But we kissed. I swore I was going to die because I felt his tongue

and I almost lost it and all I can say is thank goodness I don't have to go back to school and face him. It was like kissing a dog, seriously."

"Wow." Madison was impressed, even if one of the kisses was bordering on gross.

"I guess leaving those guys in the dust is one good reason for having moved here to Far Hills, right?" Fiona laughed. "No more DOG kisses, except for Phinnie, of course!"

"Wow, I'm jealous of you. I haven't really ever done *anything* with a guy. Well, I accept the fact that no one likes me."

"That can't be true, Madison! You are so pretty! You're just not paying attention, I bet."

Madison was embarrassed, as usual. She fought the urge to get off her bed and run away.

"It is so true, Madison," Fiona repeated. "I bet *lots* of guys like you. Didn't you say that Hart guy was chasing you around?"

"Yeah, but he's a loser."

"Still, he's a loser who's a GUY!"

"Come on, Fiona, this is so embarrassing. I get too nervous around guys. I'm the person who runs away from people, remember? Besides, the only boys who even look at me are all into wrestling and stupid boy stuff."

Fiona laughed. "Yeah, I know. Like Chet, my brother."

Fiona stayed all day long until the sun went down. It was the best day of the summer so far. It was better than Brazil. It was better than shopping. It was better than *anything*.

When Mr. Waters came by to give his daughter a lift home, Fiona whispered good-bye in Madison's ear: "Thanks for being my friend."

Fiona

We are official friends.

She has said so three times including today right here in this room. She told me when we went for ice cream last Thursday and I dropped my scoop of Raspberry Bliss on the ground. She told me in her living room the other day when we were looking at her family's old photo albums. And she told me just now. Three time's a charm, right? Mom always says that.

I think Fiona Waters is perfect and she has such a funny sense of humor and she's a little spaced out and forgetful but I forgive her. And she's experienced, too. She's kissed 2 boys! Maybe she can help me in that department?

We talked for a while today about the whole boy thing. I admitted to her that I always get crushes on older boys like the ones Mom says to stay away from. She laughed at my story from last year when the ninth grader Barry Burstein who lives up the block asked me out and I had to tell him I was still in sixth grade. Mom called his mom she was so mad but of course I was

flattered. Sometimes I see him around the neighborhood but he's still embarrassed about thinking I was older than I am.

Anyway, Fiona says that boys are no big deal and that when we're in school I'll see that for sure and even I, Madison Finn, will have a boyfriend some day.

I think the rest of the kids at Far Hills are all gonna be soooooo jealous of me because the new girl who is so cool is *already* MY friend. She and I will take electives and try out for soccer together. Fiona said so. And we'll sit next to each other at lunch. We'll maybe get into the same homeroom if we're super lucky. I hope we're lucky.

Fiona Waters is like the friend I have been waiting for all summer. She is the antidote to all this loneliness.

Madison stared at what she had written and then turned off her computer. Phinnie had fallen asleep at her feet.

"Maddie!" Mom called from the kitchen. "Your father's on the phone."

Madison hadn't even heard the telephone ring. Her mind was someplace else. On her way downstairs, she suddenly remembered something. Something important

Aimee was coming home tomorrow.

Chapter 8

Madison looked at the clock. It was just after eleven.

Aimee would be pulling into her driveway any moment now.

And Madison was still trying to sign Aimee's homemade card with just the right words. She was stuck.

She scribbled down the saying from the Girl Scouts: *Make new friends and keep the old; One is silver the other gold.* But that sounded goofy. In fact, everything Madison thought of writing just sounded terrible. It was like "Return of the Brain Freeze."

She wanted to say something important. She knew that much. Finally, she knew what to write.

This is just a card to say I missed you and I hope we will never have to be apart like this summer ever, ever again. I am lucky to call you my BFF.

Love,

Madison

P.S. I hope you missed me as much as I missed you.

She folded the card, licked the envelope and waited for Aimee's call.

There was a group of birds feeding just outside the kitchen window. The male cardinals were bright red. They were biting off the ends of sunflower seeds to feed the gray birds with the tufts on their heads, who must have been the females. They were sharing perfectly. Madison always marveled at how birds worked together to eat and talk and fly—and just *be*. She wished her mom and dad knew how to do that.

The phone rang. Madison spied the clock: noon. On the dot. Aimee was never late. Not even for phone calls.

"Is this you? Is this really and truly and absolutely YOU?" Aimee screeched. "I am just going to unpack my duffel bag and then I'm coming RIGHT OVER!"

Of course, she didn't come right over. She didn't even hang up the phone right away.

She had to say that she missed Madison when she was at camp.

Then she said that she had so many stories to share from camp.

Then she said she wished so much that Madison had been at camp.

Camp! Camp! Camp!

Madison wanted to kick "camp" in the head. First, it took her friends away from her for half the summer and now what? Were all those same friends coming home—and camp was following them back?

Madison didn't really feel like hearing about camp tents and lake trips and marshmallow roasts anymore. She had her own stories to tell, right? It wasn't as if camp had a corner on the market for making new friends. Madison had met someone new and she hadn't had to go live in a tent in the woods or attend some fancy dance camp to do it. She had met a new friend right here in Far Hills, and she was going to tell Aimee all about it.

But of course, what Madison *actually* said to Aimee was, "Cool! Can't wait to hear all about your CAMP!"

Madison felt excitement and guilt and weirdness churning inside her belly. She sat by the window to wait for Aimee's arrival. Was Aimee's hair going to be longer? Had she gotten any skinnier? Aimee didn't really eat all that much to begin with, plus she

was a ballet dancer, so that made her like a total skinny-mini. And then there was that Josh guy. Madison knew Aimee would talk about the camp counselor and of course, Madison had no boy stories of her own to compare with JOSH. What if Aimee had actually *done* something with that Josh guy? What would she say *then*?

That would be weird.

Of course, thinking through every possible hello and good-bye did Madison no good. The exact moment Madison saw Aimee cross the street, every nerve in her body stopped being nervous. She was just THRILLED.

Madison Finn exploded into a chorus of high-pitched shrieks.

"OH MY GOOOOOOOOD!"

She ran out the front door and Phin followed, barking.

Aimee and Madison practically squeezed each other to death on the front lawn.

"You look sooooo good, Maddie!" Aimee screamed. "I missed you so much!"

"So do you! I missed you so much too! Your hair is so long! You look so good, too!" Madison screamed back.

Their arms wrapped around each other like twine.

"Maddie, camp was like the best experience of my life so far I have to tell you absolutely every sin-

gle solitary detail you just won't believe how great it was oh I wish you could have been there. . . ."

Madison grinned from ear to ear. What had she been so worried about? She could survive a few of these camp stories. With Aimee in her living room again, Madison felt so much better about everything.

Seeing Aimee again, on that muggy Sunday morning after such a long dragged-out summer, was like winning first prize on a game show. It felt as good as ice cream.

"Okay-doh-kay," Aimee clucked, "so there I was and I was so afraid I wouldn't make any new friends or anything and OH MY GOD Madison I swear I was like one of the most popular dancers by the end of the summer I swear can you believe it—*me*?"

Madison didn't ever remember Aimee being so full of herself, but she kept listening. Aimee looked so happy. She was glad to know her friend was proud of being a good dancer. Everyone was allowed to toot their own horn a little, right?

Aimee was dancing around the room while she talked. "So I got the lead in *Swan Lake* there can you just die? And there was this boy dancer named Willem and he was so cute and I almost forgot!"

"What?" Madison was enraptured by what Aimee was saying and by the fact that Aimee was literally pirouetting in the living room.

"You are NOT going to believe this but Roseanne Snyder was at camp too!"

"Rose *Thorn*? Get OUT!"

"Yeah, she came for the last session. I forgot to put it in my letter." Rose *Thorn* was a nickname Madison had given to one of her classmates. Roseanne was friends with *Phony* Joanie Kenyon. They were both sidekicks to Class Enemy #1, Ivy Daly.

Ivy Daly was probably the meanest girl in Far Hills. She'd been hated by Madison, Aimee, and Egg for—well, fore*ver*. She would be attending Far Hills Junior High, too.

"Rose Thorn is such a snot! Was she in *Swan Lake* too?"

"She thinks she is all that and she is NO swan," Aimee taunted.

"And what about that Josh guy you wrote me about?" Madison asked.

"Josh? Oh well he was a counselor so that was never like a real deal or anything. And the truth is I didn't really like him after all, he just turned out to be well, not a good teacher either. SO! Forget him. Like I was saying there was this other guy Willem and he was the best dancer in the entire place. He was there when I was on pointe for the first time and he picked me up . . . I think I told you that in my letter that I started pointe, right?"

"Uh-huh." Madison nodded. She could barely get a word in. Aimee kept on talking for another ten minutes at least. Actually, she had been talking for fourteen minutes and thirty-three seconds. . . .

Thirty-nine seconds . . .

Fifty-six seconds . . .

Fifteen minutes!

Madison hated to admit it, but at a certain point she was wishing Aimee would just shut up already. It must have showed on her face.

"Is something wrong?" Aimee suddenly asked, stopping to take a breath.

"Huh?" Madison snapped back to attention. "Keep going, Aimee. I'm listening."

"But you have this weird look on your face. Are you *really* listening? I've been waiting all summer to tell you about this and OH MY GOD you would have liked all these people and the place it was so beautiful Madison it was soooooo beautiful!"

"Aimee, of course I am listening. Go ahead. I wanna know what happened, all right!"

"Okay!" she said, and spun around on her heels. "Fine!"

Madison figured Aimee must have been saving up all these words about camp. Madison *had* to let her talk or else Aimee would just bust a gut right in her living room.

I just have to be patient, Madison told herself. Aimee will listen right back when it's my turn.

And the truth was, she did.

"SO!" Aimee said after another eight minutes and ten seconds, "What about YOUR summer?"

It now felt like *hours* after Aimee had arrived and

she was finally ready to hear from the other side. Of course, Madison wasn't really sure what to say. She could tell Aimee about Brazil and the frogs. But instead, she gently said, "Well, I missed you. It was lonely here without you."

Aimee looked like she was about to bawl. She threw her arms around Madison. "OH MY GOD, I missed you too! You are so much like a real sister and I don't know what I would do if I didn't have you here. Thank you so much for listening to me. Thank you so much for being SUCH a good friend."

Madison hugged her and squeezed. When Aimee said that, it made all the "camp" talk and all the pirouettes around the living room worth it.

They spent the rest of the day together, talking. Madison eventually *did* get a chance to fill Aimee in on the different kinds of South American poisonous frogs and how not to approach a snake in the rain forest. Aimee kept telling Madison how sorry she was for monopolizing the conversation and sorry she was for being a little overly consumed by camp, but somehow, Aimee never left that subject far behind.

While they were eating wafer cookies Aimee said, "We used to have these in the barn when it rained at camp."

They painted their toenails with Madison's special brand-new orange glitter polish and all Aimee could say was, "My feet are so callused from dancing at camp."

They watched Madison's favorite love story on cable TV and Aimee said, "Did I tell you that the guy Willem was the best dancer in the entire camp?"

Madison wanted to shout back, "CAMP—SHMAMP!" But she didn't.

There was one good part about Aimee doing all the talking. The subject of Fiona never came up.

Until the phone rang—and *Aimee* picked it up.

"Hello, Finn residence," Aimee answered, laughing as she put on a fake butler voice. "Hello? You want Miss Madison? And WHOOOO may I ask is calling?"

Madison held her breath. She got all tense about Aimee answering the phone, as if Fiona meeting Aimee were *Godzilla Meets the Smog Monster*.

Madison had a feeling they wouldn't get along.

"It's Fiona. For you," Aimee handed the phone to Madison. "So who's Fiona, Maddie? Huh?"

Madison's stomach went flip-flop as it always did under pressure.

"Fiona, hey!" she grabbed the phone. Unfortunately for Madison, Fiona was in a talkative mood too. She couldn't hang up right away.

Aimee just stared and listened.

"What? Oh, you wanna hang out? . . . Well I can't. . . . Well, my friend Aimee . . . Yeah, she was the one who answered. . . . Well, she's back from dance camp and I . . . Well, we're kind of hanging out together alone right now and . . . Fiona? Look, I'll call you later."

No sooner had Madison hung up the phone than Aimee asked her for a third time, "So are you gonna tell me who Fiona is?"

Madison couldn't understand why she felt so guilty about Fiona *vs.* Aimee, but she did. She didn't understand why she always felt she had to take sides with everyone: with Mom and Dad, with friends, with *everyone*. It was always about picking sides and picking the people you liked more than other people.

Like now.

"Well, Fiona's my new friend," Madison admitted. "I met her when you were at camp."

Aimee brushed it off. "Oh, okay. Well, is she nice?"

"Yes. Very nice."

"Oh, that's cool. I can't wait to meet her." Aimee twirled around. "Anyway, you know, Maddie, I think I should probably go home now. Do you wanna get Egg and hang out tomorrow like we always do the night before school starts?"

"Yeah, I guess."

Madison was dumbfounded. Aimee wasn't asking any more Fiona questions?

"So, later, 'gator!" Aimee squeezed Madison good-bye as she made her way to the front door. She yelled out, "GOOD-BYE, MRS. FINN!" and skipped away. She really *skipped* too, which annoyed Madison a little. Aimee was a dancer.

Madison smiled and shouted out, "I'll see you tomorrow, then!"

Of course, she realized five minutes too late that she had forgotten to give Aimee her collage card. She stuffed it into her backpack so she wouldn't forget it tomorrow on the occasion of their pre-school party.

Right before bed, Madison opened up her Aimee File.

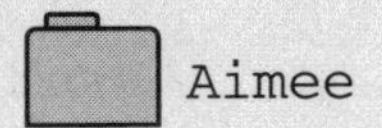

Aimee

I thought that I was doing all the changing around here, but Aimee has changed, big-time. She's not the same and she's a talking hog all of a sudden and she's not the same person I remember. I don't ever remember her being such a blabbermouth. Am I being mean by even *thinking* that?

Another change I noticed is her boobs! They are getting like really big. I didn't say that to her face, but I could see them through her T-shirt. I wonder if they hurt? She always said big boobs were like doom for a dancer. I wonder if that's true?

I hope that Aimee and Fiona can be friends. If we three get along, does that mean we have to leave Egg out? Does that destroy, like, the whole Three Musketeer thing with me, Aimee, and Egg? I had this two-second wish that maybe we *four* could be best pals, but I don't know. Maybe I'm being a hog, too. I want things my way all of a sudden.

Sometimes I just want to keep Fiona to myself. Does that make me the *friend* hog? Or is Fiona just one of those summer friends? I am confused.

Madison realized that was a topic better discussed in her Fiona File, and quickly switched back to the subject of Aimee.

I know that Aimee is my best friend in the universe and that we did the soul sisters pact thing in fourth grade and it's stupid to worry about our friendship. Right?

Madison wondered if maybe she really was still "only the lonely."

What would Bigwheels do at a time like this? She looked at her empty mailbox and felt extra lonely.

Chapter 9

It was 1 A.M.

Mom was fast asleep.

Phin was fast asleep.

But Madison was wide awake. Madison couldn't remember being up this late since the year Mom and Dad let her stay up for New Year's Eve when Mom was on the road making *Documentary of a Documentary*, or something like that.

My mind is racingracingracing, Madison thought to herself. It was super-hot, too. Mom had turned down the air-conditioning because she claimed it was supposed to rain. The bedroom fan wasn't working properly. Madison felt sweaty and way too conscious. She'd much rather be dreaming than facing this reality: it was the early morning before the night before the start of seventh grade.

SEVENTH GRADE.

It was all Madison could think about. Her insides were jumping beans. Her head thumped. She swore she could smell smells stronger than before. It was like the whole world was changing.

SEVENTH GRADE.

Wasn't that enough to keep anyone awake?

Madison had spent the last part of the summer worrying about her parents, her friends, and her slow death from boredom, and just now—with twenty-four hours to go—she realized that the thing she was probably most worried about all along was junior high.

Around 5 A.M., Madison finally did fall asleep. At long last she was wiped out by all her thinking. She slept for almost six hours, too, but then Mom finally woke her up.

The first thing sleepy Madison did was check her e-mailbox. To her surprise, she discovered a bunch of messages from a bunch of people she hadn't expected to hear from.

FROM	SUBJECT
✉ dELiA's	Super Savings—PLUS!
✉ jefffinn	I'M HOME!

wetwinz   is this you???

Bigwheels   sorry

The message from dELiA's was an even bigger discount promise on their latest sale. Madison was psyched, until she deleted the message by mistake.

JeffFinn, a.k.a. Dad, sent news from his Far Hills apartment. He was home at last and he wanted to take Madison to dinner the first night of school on Tuesday. It would be special in honor of his junior high school girl. Sometimes Daddy said the sappiest things. Madison couldn't wait to see him. It had been a month, after all. She missed his hamburgers almost as much as his hugs.

The next message was from Wetwinz. *Fiona* had sent mail—*finally!* Fiona and Chet both had screen names that were variations on the words "we twins." Chet's screen identity ended in *s* and Fiona's ended in *z*.

From: Wetwinz
To: MadFinn
Subject: is this you???
Date: Mon, 4 Sept 9:31 AM

Happy day before school, Maddie.

Can I call you that now that we're friends?

I have a lot to do w/mom and Chet before school but I'll see you tomorrow at Far Hills okay? I am so SCARED for everything that's new but I am also so excited. Do you know what I mean? I am more excited because we are friends now, too. Have fun with Aimee and Egg tonight. You said you guys always celebrate together on the night before school, right? Sorry I can't be there with you!

Bye, Maddie!!!
Love, Fiona

Madison wished Fiona could be here, even if that meant breaking tradition a little bit. She wondered how Egg and Aimee would react if Fiona turned their threesome into a foursome. It wouldn't be fair, of course. Egg had wanted his pal Drew officially included in a lot of things, too, but Drew usually got left out. The three best friends wanted to hang on to their trio for as long as possible with no strangers included or invited.

Was seventh grade going to change all that?

Madison's last message was from Bigwheels.

From: Bigwheels
To: MadFinn

Subject: school
Date: Mon, 4 Sept 10:32 AM

I think maybe you sent me a message too last week and it got zapped. Sorry. Lemme know. And resend it if you still have it.

BTW I start school government next week so I may actually be a little busy so please don't mind if I can't e-m right away. I promise will write ASAP. Bye!

p.s. pls. Are you angry about something? Why is your screen name MAD? Bye!
p.p.s. Oh, did I tell you that I like to write poems? Ok, here is one for you for the first day of school. I'm always scared about new things. RU?

Scared

When toes curl
When hands sweat
When eyes twitch
When you're not set
Scared of people making fun
Scared of summer being done
Scared of new

```
Scared of old
Scared of always being told
What to do and who to see
Do you agree?
Are you scared like me?
```

Madison couldn't believe that other people out there in the middle of the world were as freaked out about starting junior high as she was.

Was Far Hills Junior High just a bunch of scaredy-cats like her?

She closed the window on her computer. She couldn't think about being scared now. She was sure Aimee and Egg weren't scared! She made a mental note to send Bigwheels an e-mail later on. She wanted to thank her for the poem.

Ever since they had gotten out of kindergarten, Madison, Aimee, and Egg had been celebrating together on the night right before school and here it was all over again. Their moms were the ones who had really started the tradition and the three friends had picked it up a few years back.

One year they went roller-skating. Another time they camped out in a tent in the backyard. After such a long tradition, they had gotten superstitious about the whole thing.

Egg got to the Finn house first tonight. The dog jumped him.

"Phin you are a bad, bad doggy! Get back!" Egg joked, but then he tickled the spot behind Phin's sen-

sitive ears and Phin turned to Jell-O.

Egg definitely had a love-hate-love relationship with Phinnie.

"Hello there, Walter Diaz!" Madison greeted Egg at the door with a smack on the back.

"Hello there, Madison Finn."

Egg was about to smack back, even harder, when Aimee rushed up and threw her arms around him instead.

"Get off me!" Egg screamed. Of course, he was happy to see her, he just wasn't into any kind of squeezing or hugging. "You're sick," he added.

Aimee laughed and hugged Madison instead. Then she twirled around, waving her arms down toward the ground. She was wearing her pointe shoes.

Madison gasped. "That's them?"

"Aren't they magic?" Aimee got up on pointe and showed off her balance on one toe. She was good at showing off even in the strangest places.

Egg made a face at Aimee's feet. "That's just messed. How do you get up on your toenails like that? Gross me."

Aimee and Madison laughed and threw their arms around each other again.

It had been three months since they had last hung out. Madison, Aimee, and Egg were back together again at last. For a split second Madison considered whether she really should have gotten

Fiona to join them, but Fiona had said she had other plans and Madison left it at that. This was no time to feel guilty.

Outside, it was a perfect summer night, so the trio parked their butts on the Finn patio as Mom lit a few citronella candles, and passed out popcorn and root beer.

Madison made Phin do a few stupid pet tricks like fetching the hose, rolling over in the grass, and sitting on the command "park it." Basically Phin did whatever Madison wanted him too. It was entertaining.

"So what are you guys most nervous about this year?" Aimee asked all of a sudden.

Silence. The bug zapper zapped, but no one seemed to have an answer for Aimee's question.

"Nothing, *nada*, not a thing," Egg finally replied. "What's to be nervous about? Bunch of losers mixed in with another bunch of geeks. I'm not different from the rest of the crowd, right?"

Madison chuckled. "Except that you're King Geek, remember?"

"Oh yeah. Where's my crown, Miss Loser? Did you borrow it again?"

"You guys are out of control," Aimee said, interrupting. "I was talking about school stuff like classes and, you know, teachers, and I have heard some scary stories about the amount of homework—like we thought sixth grade was bad but I have a feeling

seventh grade is just worse. My brothers say that it's evil."

Aimee had four older brothers: Roger, Billy, Dean, and Doug. They had all been through seventh grade and survived just fine, so Madison imagined they were exaggerating for Aimee's benefit.

"What's their definition of *evil*, Aimee?" Madison inquired.

Egg spoke up, "Uh, I do believe that next to the word *evil* in the dictionary you will find a picture of Aimee herself, yeah."

Aimee faked being mad for a minute and then she hauled off and gave Egg a knuckle noogie.

"Owwwwwwch!" Egg screamed, kicking her in the shin.

"Boys and girls, please stop this fighting," Madison announced like a flight attendant. "In case of emergency, your seat cushions can be used as flotation devices."

They all cracked up.

"Hey, has anyone seen Ivy Daly this summer?" Egg asked out of the blue.

"Oh, puke me!" Madison yelped. "Are you kidding me?"

"I hung out with Ivy's BFF for a week," Aimee said. "Roseanne can't *jeté* or pirouette to save her life!"

Madison faked a scream. "POISON Ivy? Aahhh!"

"I don't know how it's possible but I almost

forgot about her," Madison said. "*She* is the one whose picture is in the dictionary next to *evil*, Egg."

"Madison *vs.* Poison. Sounds like a good wrestling match." Egg snickered.

Hating Ivy officially had started in fourth grade, a year after Ivy moved to town and moved into their elementary school. As third graders, she and Madison had totally bonded. They spent every afternoon together doing homework and playing at the park and all the things that new friends do.

Then things changed.

Egg pulled on Ivy's braids one day in recess and she tripped him in the corridor and then he beaned her in kickball and things got *way* out of hand. Madison tried to stick up for her new friend, but no one listened. And that was when Ivy spread an awful rumor that Madison had cheated on a math test and soon everyone in the fourth grade was whispering and after that the principal got involved. . . .

Any mortal enemy of Madison's automatically became a mortal enemy of Aimee's and Egg's, too.

The worst backstabbing kicked in the year before when Madison went so far as to nickname Ivy "Poison." Of course she never said that to her face.

"I never thought about this before but Poison Ivy just might ruin seventh grade," Madison complained. "She and her stupid sidekicks Rose *Thorn* and *Phony* Joanie."

"Ivy won't ruin *anything* if we have anything to

say about it," Aimee said. "I mean I know I'll whup her and Roseanne in dance troupe tryouts. And you're way smarter than they are, Maddie. That's something to be glad for, right?"

"Yeah, Ivy's hot but she's a major math moron, too," Egg said.

Madison and Aimee said at the same time, "EGG!"

"She is a hottie! I may be against her politically speaking, but I'm not blind!" Egg argued. "She's good-looking."

Aimee jumped all over him. "Those three witches are off-limits for friendship and crushes. Egg, you don't mingle with the enemy no matter what, got it? I mean it, Egg. You are totally not allowed to crush on any of them."

Why was Aimee being so bossy toward Egg? Madison wondered. Egg didn't seem to mind, so she laughed it off, too. Still, it seemed that Aimee really had changed a little. And here, on the night before seventh grade, she was changing a little bit *more*.

"So what homeroom are you in anyway, Maddie?" Aimee asked.

"2A." Madison said.

Egg piped up, "Hey, I'm in 2A too."

Aimee was bummed out. "Then why did they put *me* in 2B?"

The very logical Egg answered her. "Alphabet,

Aimee. A through F is in Room A. Then G through O or something is Room B, and the rest are in Room C. Something like that. They do it all on the computer."

"How do you guys know?" Aimee asked.

Madison joked, "Hey, I think they stuck you in 2B just to torture you, Aimee."

"They finally figured out how to separate you two!" Egg added.

"That isn't funny, Egg. I don't want to be in a different homeroom than you guys. That isn't fair."

"We'll live, Aimee," Egg said. "We'll probably have all our other classes together. Besides, you should feel lucky you're not in Room A. The lovely Poison Ivy is in there!"

Madison put her hand on Aimee's shoulder. "We'll have every other class together, I bet we will."

"I guess," Aimee agreed halfheartedly. She seemed dejected.

Everyone was a smidge more worried than they wanted to admit.

"You're not really upset, Aimee, are you?" Madison asked.

"Yeah, I am. I'm bummed."

Madison wanted to make Aimee feel better. That's what BFFs were for, after all. She remembered Aimee's collage card, the one she'd been making for most of the month of August. It was still in her backpack.

"You made this?" Aimee whimpered. "You made this for me?"

Madison nodded and Aimee sniffled. She was *almost* crying.

"You guys, I feel like I have been waiting for this moment all my life, waiting to get older, to get into junior high, to start dating finally and become a good dancer and get smarter and just start moving up in the world in general. All my brothers are major successes in everything they do and I have to be that way too.

"Now the day is here. Seventh grade is here. We're like, grown-up now. We have to deal with things now. My brothers are telling me that in seventh grade all your friends change and no one likes you. Junior high is all about being popular."

Madison took a deep breath. "Aimee?" she asked quietly.

"Mmm-uh-huh."

"Well, what are you wearing tomorrow?"

"What?"

"What are you wearing tomorrow, Aimee?"

"I dunno. Clothes."

They couldn't help but laugh at that one.

"Well, I'll probably wear my capri pants and that yellow shirt I got last spring with the embroidery, you know the one with the little ties? Or maybe my flower skirt and a T-shirt."

Madison told Aimee that she would wear the

same exact shirt, only in lilac. Then they could be alike but not exactly the same so no one could accuse them of being copycats or anything.

"You should wear those cool sandals, too, with the red straps," Madison added. "They would look so good with that shirt."

Egg was not especially interested in his friends' fashion plans so he said his good-nights.

"See you in the land of the lost," he said, joking about the halls of Far Hills Junior High, where they'd meet up again tomorrow. "Thanks for the eats, Maddie. Too bad all the Pop-Tarts were gone."

They laughed and waved and then Aimee stayed for another hour with Madison planning their outfits and outfitting themselves with a plan.

Madison typed up their list into a new file.

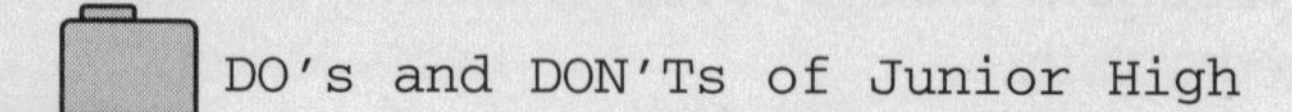

Do's and Don'ts: Day One
by Madison Francesca Finn
and Aimee Anne Gillespie

DO coordinate your new school outfit with your BFF the night before 7th grade starts.

DON'T wear anything see-through and don't wear a dark-colored bra under a white shirt. No glitter barrettes either or anything too flashy. Blending in is the best plan.

DO put your clothes out the night before school so you don't have to run around like a freak on the next morning looking for something cute to wear.

DON'T wear anything white on the first day unless of course you have a good tan in which case you should wear white on the first day and every day after that until the tan fades away.

DO bring most of what the faculty put on the school supply list: new notebooks, sharpened pencils, and pens. You will feel like a big loser if you don't have something to write with.

DO put all your stuff into a knapsack or backpack or whatever you call it.

DON'T use the same backpack as you did in sixth grade. People will notice.

DO eat breakfast before school starts on the first day but make sure you don't get food on your new outfit.

DO bring lunch money or a lunch bag. You need food to keep awake on the first day of junior high. There's a lot of important stuff to pay attention to.

DON'T eat anything that looks like it's moving.

DON'T chat with the lunch lady or lunch guy.

DO write down your school locker combination on your palm so you don't forget it.

DON'T move into your school locker until you have been at school for at least a week. Test the locker area to make sure that you are okay with your locker location, after which you can paste up pictures and whatever else you need to paste up.

Madison kept typing their list right up until the moment when Aimee's ride came to take her home.

"Madison! Aimee!" Mom yelled out after the door buzzed.

Aimee's oldest brother, Roger, was standing at the front door.

"Hey, Maddie Finn, what's up?" Roger smiled from the porch step. His teeth sparkled. Madison didn't remember him being so . . . *cute*. Had something about him changed too? He had the same thick blond hair and brown eyes that Aimee had. But he looked different. Very different . . .

"So we'll meet in the morning and walk to school, right?" Aimee gushed. "I missed you so much Maddie and I'm so glad to be back and right here."

Madison choked a little. Aimee was squeezing pretty hard.

"Okay, break it up you two." Roger joked,

pulling on Aimee's arm. "Mom wants you to get a little sleep before school, Aim."

Aimee threw her arms around Madison's mom, too. "Thank you, Mrs. Finn! I missed you too. 'Bye!"

She skipped down the stairs, as usual.

"See you tomorrow, Aimee!" Madison waved back. "See you in seventh grade!"

Chapter 10

The first person Madison spotted in seventh grade homeroom was Ivy Daly.

Of course.

Since 2A was last name letters A through F, Ivy Daly belonged there, just as Egg had said. She was standing at the classroom door chatting with some blond guy Madison didn't recognize. He had probably attended the other middle school and probably was named Biff or Boff or maybe Doof. Madison was trying hard not to stereotype other people too much—but it was a challenge. Mere moments into the first school day, Ivy was moving in for the kill on the cutest boy in school.

The first bell hadn't even rung yet.

"Look at her, trying too hard as always," Egg

coughed. He whispered in Madison's ear, "But she looks good, right?"

"NO!" Madison punched him. "Shhhh!"

Madison never understood why Ivy had been voted Princess of the Middle School Dance last spring, since as far as she could tell every single girl in school hated her guts. Egg claimed Ivy had bribed fifth graders with chocolate to cast their votes for her.

Madison hated Ivy for a million reasons, but there was a teeny-tiny part of her that was a teeny-tiny bit jealous, too. She was jealous of the way Ivy knew how to get all the attention. It was like she could walk into a room and suck out all the energy. She was always the teacher's pet. People listened to her, and she never looked lonely.

"I am sorry, but she is just a tease." Egg elbowed Madison, shaking his head. "She's popular like . . . in her dreams."

Madison looked at the clock. It was 8:04 and seventh grade was two bells away from starting. As kids rushed into the classroom, Madison and Egg said "hello" and "how was your summer" to everyone they'd missed since June. Egg's friend Drew was in this homeroom 2A too, and he and Egg started chattering about Palm Pilots and RAM as soon as they spotted each other. The entire classroom was a flurry of activity. Plus, no one knew where their lockers were located yet, so everyone had piles of stuff to carry around with them.

The first bell rang.

Madison wondered how Fiona was doing on her first day at Far Hills. She hadn't spoken to her since the other night. Of course Fiona and Chet were probably together, so Madison didn't think Fiona would feel totally alone.

Egg poked Madison's side to get her attention. "Drew's having a party Friday," he said.

"Well, my parents are," Drew continued. "Like a start-of-school-and-end-of-summer party. A barbecue. It's the third year we've done it."

"Oh that's nice," said Madison, flashing a smile. "Is that an invitation?"

Drew smiled. "Yuh. Of course. Yeah."

Egg chimed in, looking at his neon watch as he always did. "Second bell will go off in exactly three seconds . . . three . . . two . . ."

The second bell rang.

By the time homeroom had ended, teachers were running back and forth, up and down the aisles handing out dittos and schedules and maps. Far Hills Junior High was big, probably about four times the size of Far Hills Elementary. The kids needed a major map to find their way. Even with directions, most seventh graders wandered down the wrong hallways and found themselves trapped on the opposite side of the building from where their next class was being held.

Madison thought her map looked like it had been written in Japanese.

"I can't read maps to save my life," Madison moaned when she got her pack of multicolored pages. "I have no sense of direction—EGG!"

There was so much to learn and absorb. Where was she going to be going? How would she get there?

Madison's schedule said: ENGLISH, Room 407. Egg had math on the second floor with Drew, so when homeroom bell rang, they waved good-bye.

Of course, there was no elevator, so Madison went immediately to the jam-packed stairwell, grabbed the banister, and inched her way up two flights. When she got up there, she looked high and low for the classroom.

"Hey, Finnster!" a voice called out from down the hall. Madison's eyes searched for the source.

A very handsome guy with little black glasses, hair that swept up off his face, and dimples, walked up to her and smiled. He was *awfully* cute for a seventh grader, Madison thought. *Awfully* cute.

"Madison, is it you? How are you?"

Madison thought she recognized the voice, but she couldn't place the face. "I'm sorry. . . ." she started to say, blushing a little bit.

"It's Hart. Hart Jones! Remember? When we caught that sunfish? My family moved but we moved back again. Funny, huh?"

Madison froze. *This hunk was HART?* Finnster should have been a dead giveaway. Hart called her that in second grade.

"H-h-h-hello, H-h-h-hart," she stuttered, barely getting the words out. "Gee . . . uh . . . see ya!" she made a U-turn in the opposite direction. She told herself she was speeding off to first period, but of course she was just running away as she always did.

"Hola, Señorita Finn!" another voice called out. It was Mrs. Diaz, the best Spanish teacher in the world and mother to Walter, otherwise known as Egg Diaz.

"Hello . . . uhhh . . . *hola*, Mrs. . . . uhhh . . . Señora Diaz." Madison said with a lot of effort. She knew maybe ten Spanish words and most of those didn't even count because they were curse words she'd learned on cable TV.

"Cómo era tu verano?" Egg's mother wanted to have a conversation in Spanish in the middle of the hallway and Madison was NOT prepared.

"Uh . . . see you later, Mrs. Diaz. I have class. . . ." Madison fumbled for the words. *"Ahora . . . class . . . Oh, hasta la vista, Señora!"*

The first bell rang.

Madison's eyes scanned the doorways for her classroom number. She saw 4D. Then she saw 4C. These looked like language labs, not English class-rooms.

The clock was ticking. The hallways were empty-ing. Madison felt her stomach doing its usual flip-flop as she desperately looked for the right room. These were all letters! Where were the *numbers*?

"Excuse me," she suddenly asked a male teacher

who was about to lock his classroom door, "Excuse me, where is Room 407?"

He chuckled and said "Ooooooh" and Madison knew she was in deep trouble. "Ooooooh," he said again, "Miss, that's over in the other building."

"The *other* building?"

"Yes. You go down those stairs there, all the way across the quad out there, and then through two sets of glass doors, and then up the middle stairwell, and then across the top floor, which is four, and then there are a whole bunch of rooms sort of kitty-corner. . . ."

Madison's head was spinning.

The second bell rang.

"Good luck!" he trilled, slamming his classroom door.

Madison realized that she was the only person left standing in the hallway—without a hall pass.

"Great going, Madison," she said out loud to herself, on the verge of tears. Then, she ran. She ran fast, too. So fast, in fact, that she got grabbed by another teacher in the other building who gave her a warning for running.

"Just because you're in junior high school now young lady doesn't mean you can break all the rules and do whatever you please," the woman said. Madison prayed this crabby lady wasn't going to be one of her teachers. She just grit her teeth and kept moving ahead.

By the time she finally did make it to 407, class

was already underway. She was the last to arrive.

Madison was convinced that *her* nightmares were coming true. At least this one didn't involve dogs and frogs.

On the upside, English class looked promising. The teacher went out of his way to get Madison to relax once she finally took her seat.

"Why don't you take a few breaths and get your bearings. Class, I'm Mr. Gibbons and this is seventh-grade English."

Madison wasn't sure she knew *where* her bearings were right about now. She didn't see Aimee anywhere. And Egg wasn't here, either. Madison was alone in this English class with none other than Poison Ivy and a bunch of her followers.

Mr. Gibbons handed out the "syllabus." Madison glanced at it, expecting to find the usual grammar page assignments, vocabulary lists, and all that razzamatazz. But what she saw was something very different. At the top of the page was "Mr. Gibbons," and the class unit number, and then in the very center of page three:

Expect the unexpected.

"Okay, class, who can tell me what we'll be studying this year," Mr. Gibbons asked. He was parading around the room looking for guinea pigs disguised as seventh graders.

Madison blinked at the page and . . . of course . . . started to over-think.

Seventh grade had already thrown her about four curve balls and it was only nine in the morning.

And that's when Fiona walked into the room.

Madison almost blurted her name out, "Fi—" but she stopped.

As Fiona took a seat in the next row, Madison leaned over to hand her a copy of the page Mr. Gibbons had passed out.

Expect the unexpected.

"He seems cool," Madison whispered.

"Seeing you in my English class is unexpected," Fiona said, pointing down at her page as if she was answering a question. "I guess I already expected the unexpected here."

Brrrrrrrrrrrring!

"Huh?" Madison smiled. As far as she could hear, the only thing that could be expected at Far Hills were the bells. Every time Madison got comfortable in a seat . . .

Brrrrrrrrrrrring!

These twenty-minute first-day classes were giving her a headache.

Chapter 11

After English, Fiona and Madison blabbed between bells and agreed to meet later in the lunchroom. They'd be serving some kind of snack to keep the kids' motors running.

"This new school is so weird! California was way more mellow." Fiona tossed her head back and the beads on her braids clinked. "So I'll see you later, then? Meet me at one of the tables."

Fiona was one of the few people Madison was seeing in classes. It seemed like Aimee and Madison had been officially "separated." Her BFF was nowhere to be seen.

Madison went to the computer tech labs next, where she saw Egg and Drew again. Of course, they

were goofing around at their adjacent terminals and paying absolutely no attention to her. Madison doodled on her tech schedule, drawing little stick people with giant heads.

"Hey, Maddie," Egg elbowed her from the side, "Can you believe we're really in junior high? Just look at these computers!"

Their new computer teacher Mrs. Wing was telling the class "to be super-careful with the 'mice' and the keyboards."

Mice?

"Isn't she cool?" Egg said as they walked out of the tech lab. Egg always fell for every new female teacher he ever had. He had been doing that since Miss Jeremiah's kindergarten class.

Madison was grateful that at least someone was having a good day, even if it was Egg. Today was not turning out the way she'd planned it inside her head.

Madison sighed and looked at her map again. Lucky for her, computer and her next class, science, were near each other, so she probably wouldn't get lost again. But first, she had to eat.

The bell rang.

Madison walked into the cafeteria. It was as busy as the mall on Saturday. Kids were everywhere, talking, screaming, hugging, and eating little containers of yogurt, bagels, and fruit cups. Madison searched the sea of faces. Where was Aimee? Where was Fiona?

From across the room, she saw Fiona sitting at a

table with some other people who Madison couldn't see—*at first*. As soon as Madison started walking closer to the table, her stomach flip-flopped.

Fiona was gesturing for Madison to sit in a seat next to—*Poison Ivy*?

"Hey, Madison! How was your day so far!" Fiona blurted. "Sit here!"

"Yeah, Madison sit here," Poison Ivy groaned, not moving over. Rose Thorn and Phony Joanie laughed but Fiona didn't catch what was going on. She kept right on talking, unaware of what was happening. She was being a little spacey again.

"Madison, do you know Ivy and Roseanne and Joan?"

Madison stared and nodded. "Yes, yes, and yes."

By now, Ivy was grinning. "Fiona, we've known each other since third grade, actually. Right, Madison?"

Madison's head screamed, "RUN AWAY!" Fortunately, it was at that exact moment that Aimee bumped her from behind.

"We saved you a seat over here, Maddie."

Madison looked at Fiona and then at Aimee. Poison Ivy was ruining everything about lunch.

"Look Fiona, thanks for the invite, but I have friends waiting for me over there. I'll see you around, okay?"

"Madison?" Fiona's jaw dropped. "Madison? Where are you going? I thought you said . . ."

She stood up to stop her, but Madison had already hustled away.

"Check you out! Talking with the enemy!" Egg teased as Madison passed by his table.

"Hey, Madison," Drew called out sheepishly, "What's up?"

Madison didn't even hear Drew. She made a bee-line for the long orange table at the back of the room.

"Was *that* the Fiona girl who called you the other night?" Aimee asked, sliding in beside her.

Madison nodded. "How can she be sitting with Ivy, Rose, and Joan?"

"You won't believe this but that girl Fiona's in my science block. Maddie, she is a major poser. I wouldn't be so worried if I were—"

"Excuse me?" Madison couldn't believe Aimee would say something like that, especially when she knew how Madison felt about her newest friend. "What do you mean by 'poser'? She is not a poser. She's nice. She's my new friend, Aimee."

Aimee rolled her eyes. "Well, I don't know. She just is. Look at her. Why do you think she's sitting with *them*?"

Madison sneaked a look back at Poison and the gang. Fiona was drinking a juice.

"What about the way she looks?" Aimee said.

"Since when did you judge people like that? What are you talking about, Aimee? She's new. She doesn't know Ivy is poisonous."

"Hey, I'm not judging her! Come on, Maddie!"

Just then, Egg walked up to the orange table. "Hey, Maddie, can you set me up with that one with the braids? If you ask me, she's pretty cute."

"No one asked you anything, Egghead." Aimee threw a grape at his head.

Drew didn't say much. He just laughed whenever Egg laughed.

Madison turned her body a little so she could spy on Fiona's table some more. What was going on?

It was like this whole other Fiona was sitting there with Ivy.

It was like this whole other Aimee was sitting here with Madison.

Aimee, as usual, kept right on talking, changing the subject, too. She was good at that. "Okay Maddie, you have to tell me about your classes. I am so bummed that we don't have English or science together. How did that happen? Who did the stupid schedules and let's go complain!"

"I don't know," Madison mumbled.

Aimee told Madison about her science teacher who she claimed was close to a hundred. "I swear! She can barely stand at the front of the classroom to write on the marker boards. And her element chart looks like it was made in 1950 or something, it's falling off the wall. And she wears those orthopedic shoes you know the ones I mean. . . ."

"She's really old," Drew added, simply.

This time, Madison was the one who rolled her eyes. "Well, old doesn't mean anything except that she knows a lot more. So that's good, right? You guys are so obnoxious."

Aimee ignored that comment and kept right on talking. "Hey, Egg, who do you have for science?"

"I haven't had science yet," he grunted, devouring a sesame bagel.

"Hey, Maddie, you won't believe who I saw in the hallway by the way!" Aimee said.

"Hart?" Madison couldn't keep herself from grinning even though Aimee had her a little annoyed.

"Did you see him too?" Aimee shrieked.

"Hart *Jones*?" Egg asked.

"Hart Jones?" Drew repeated.

"Yes, are you deaf? Hart Jones." Madison said, not revealing any more information than that. She lowered her voice. "He looks *really* different though."

"Different?" Aimee shrieked again. "He's a babe!"

"Shhhhhh!" Madison shushed her. "What if he's around here?"

"If you don't want him, I'll take him," Aimee joked. "Drew, don't you remember that drip who used to always follow Madison around and stuff? He was even nerdier than Egg!" She threw another grape at Egg's head.

"Of course I know Hart Jones, Aimee," Drew piped up. "He's my cousin."

Egg laughed, hard. "Ha! Nice one, Aimee!"

"Oopsie!" Aimee gasped and covered her mouth.

She and Madison burst into peals of laughter. "NO WAY!"

Egg picked up his snack tray and pulled on Drew's shirt. "Let's go. They've crossed over into the girl zone. I can't handle this."

Aimee smiled again. "Mad and Hart, sitting in a tree, K-I-S-S-I-N-G."

Now Drew was the one who looked a little confused.

Madison grabbed a grape and threw it at Aimee. Of course, Madison's typical luck caused the grape to ricochet off Aimee's shoulder and into the assistant principal, Mrs. Bonnie Goode, who happened to be walking by at that exact moment. She shot a look in the direction of the orange table and Egg almost laughed milk out of his nose, it was so funny.

"Nice way to start the school year, right?" he cracked after the A.P. had walked away. Drew chuckled too.

Aimee finished up her yogurt and the four of them went off to the Assembly Hall. One more double period and the Far Hills seventh graders were free. Seventh grade had started with a whoosh and a bang.

Of course, Fiona had eaten lunch with THE

ENEMY, but the more she thought about it, the more Madison realized that Fiona had no idea *who* was enemy and who was friendly in this war zone. All's fair in lunch and war, so if Fiona had no facts, she had no way to know that girl was evil.

It was up to Madison to help Fiona see the poison in Poison Ivy.

She'd send Fiona an e-mail later on about it.

Chapter 12

Madison, Aimee, and Egg walked home together after school let out. Drew lived on the other side of town.

It was one of those hot and humid days that makes you sweat behind your knees. Egg complained, "Why did I wear long pants?"

"So no one would have to look at your ugly legs, obviously," Aimee laughed. They chased each other up the street.

Madison had searched for Fiona before leaving school, thinking maybe they'd walk home together too, but she was nowhere to be found. Madison hadn't seen Chet anywhere in school today, either. Far Hills was a big place. Of course, lucky

Madison had seen Ivy in every single hallway, classroom and girls' bathroom. Poison Ivy was really contagious.

Aimee dropped Madison off on her porch and continued up the street, skipping.

Phin was at the front door the moment Madison entered the house.

"Wanna go O-U-T?"

They were just going to cruise around the lawn for a quickie, but Madison walked a little farther up the street. Soon she found herself at the corner of Ridge Road, right by Fiona's.

"Hey, look where we ended up, Phin," Madison said with mock surprise. "Should we go see Fiona?"

"Rowrrroooo!" he howled. Madison took that as a "yes." She needed to see her new friend. She wanted a chance to apologize for her behavior in the cafeteria. She hadn't meant to run away that time—but she *had*.

As Madison approached number five Ridge Road, she saw Fiona sitting on her front porch. She was alone, which was good. Madison didn't feel like dealing with her twin brother in the middle of this mess.

How would Madison apologize? She figured that Fiona might be extra-understanding, because Fiona knew Madison was in the habit of fleeing when things got weird and that had definitely been one of those weird moments.

"Fiona," Madison practiced what she would say.

"Fiona, I am very sorry for leaving you there today with the enemy. You see, Ivy Daly is not exactly a friend of mine. She—"

Madison froze.

Ivy Daly was standing there on Fiona's porch.

Poison Ivy must have been inside or out of sight when Madison had first glanced that way.

She turned around and ran home as fast as she could. No one saw her great escape.

"Hey! My junior high schooler!" Mom cheered as Madison rushed inside. "Well, how was it?"

Madison was flushed. She dropped into a chair.

"What is it honey? Are you okay? What happened?"

Madison's dramatic entrance had Mom worried she was sick or something.

"Mom, do I have a sign on my head that says 'Keep Back 100 Feet'?"

Mom leaned in closer and gently grabbed Madison's arms. "What happened, sweetie? What happened at school?"

Madison looked up at her mother. She didn't want to cry. She told herself not to cry. She didn't want to yell, either, not now. Her feelings were jumbled and the words wouldn't come out like she wanted them to come out.

Madison had never, ever lied to Mom before now. In fact, she always shared *everything* with Mom. But right now, she couldn't tell her the truth.

Madison was too embarrassed by today's events. So she lied.

"Nothing's wrong, Mom, not really. School was okay. I like it. I like my classes. My teachers are okay. I saw everyone. I'm gonna go now."

"Madison?"

She just didn't feel like getting into it, not one little bit. She was too ashamed, too devastated, too woozy. She went up to her room and curled up in a ball with Phin.

An hour or so later, the phone rang.

"Mad-i-son!" Mom bellowed from downstairs. From the pinched sound of her voice, Madison knew who was on the line. Dad.

"Hey," she cooed as she took the receiver. Madison needed Dad badly.

He told her to be out front by five o'clock. Tonight was their very special dinner and Madison missed Dad so much and she needed his moral support—now more than ever. Plus, Dad was making Madison's favorite thing on the planet: french fries and steak. She'd first had it last year when she went to Paris with her parents—before the big D. She kept a postcard of the Eiffel Tower up on her wall to remind her what it was like when they were all together.

"I can't believe he makes you *steak frites*!" Mom groaned. Mom hadn't eaten meat in four years, a fact she was happy to share whenever the subject of beef came up. She didn't understand how Madison

could be an animal lover and eat meat, too, but Madison usually avoided that conversation. She liked animals but she just wasn't willing to give up burgers—what was the problem with that?

Because Madison hadn't seen Dad in so long, she tried to fix up her hair to look extra nice. She borrowed Mom's yellow sundress, too.

"Why do you want to wear this, honey? It's too big for you," Mom stated, zipping up the back. Madison had to wear a white T-shirt underneath so you couldn't see anything.

"I dunno, Mom," she answered. "I just feel like wearing a yellow dress, that's all."

"It actually looks like the sundress Fiona was wearing the other day," Mom observed. Of course, Madison had known that when she picked it out of Mom's closet.

Dad arrived a few minutes after five, but Madison wasn't phased. Dad was always late. It made Mom unhappy that he didn't understand "being on time."

Mom had staked out the front porch with Phin at her side.

So as soon as he pulled into the driveway, Madison ran for Dad's car. She liked it much better when Mom and Dad didn't have to talk to each other face-to-face. Right after the divorce, for about a month, Madison wanted nothing more than Mom and Dad to get back together. Now, she'd rather see

them on two separate islands in the middle of the Pacific Ocean.

"Gee, Maddie, your hair looks so pretty," Dad said as soon as Madison hopped into his car. "And isn't that a nice color yellow dress."

Daddy always noticed those things. Madison smiled. She wouldn't admit that the dress was really Mom's. As usual, she went way out of her way to avoid the subject of "Mom."

When they got to Dad's apartment, it smelled funky, but Madison didn't say anything. He was never there, after all. In Dad's townhouse loft, Madison actually had her own room, so she rushed in to visit it. She didn't have many things, just a photograph of her, Aimee, and Egg taken the summer before at the beach; copies of *The Phantom Tollbooth* and *Harry Potter and the Sorcerer's Stone*; a Magic 8-Ball; and one of Gramma's hand crocheted afghans.

Dinner was served about an hour after they arrived. Daddy talked nonstop about his new Internet start-up company. Sometimes Dad would get so caught up in talking about himself and his job that he would throw out all these big computer programming words Madison did not understand. She kept listening though. She really wanted to know what the words meant.

Madison felt so safe in Dad's house, watching him cook. He was a better cook than Mom, at least.

The steak was yummy and Madison over-salted her fries too, as always. Of course, they had ice cream for dessert. It was Madison's favorite flavor: Cherry Garcia.

"So, honey, I have been doing all the talking tonight."

Of course this was nothing new. He *always* did a lot of talking. Just like Aimee.

"Maddie? It's your turn to talk now. Tell me about Brazil."

Madison told Dad how they went on a big plane; then a smaller plane; and then by boat all the way out to this small village.

"Mom's making that frog-u-mentary, eh?" Daddy joked.

"Yeah," Madison laughed out loud. She realized they were discussing the untouchable subject of Mom, but she continued. "I think Mom has to go back in a week or something, too. I dunno. You guys are both out of town a lot these days, I guess."

"Yeah, well, it's not forever, Maddie. Hey, so tell me all about your new school. How's junior high?"

Madison said something about "too many people" and "too much work." Daddy grinned and handed her a small, wrapped gift. "Here's a little something for the *second* day of school. Maybe it'll be a little less overwhelming. And a toast, of course, to my big girl. I really can't believe you're in junior high school. Your old man feels *old*."

Madison opened the box. Inside, Dad had bought her a pair of earrings with teeny moonstones in the middle of teeny silver-wire flowers. They were beautiful. Madison modeled them immediately.

When Madison was ten, Daddy had given her a moonstone necklace because, he said, moonstones had special powers. She had worn it everywhere until one day she lost it in the Far Hills public pool. Egg had tried to dive in after it, but the pool filter sucked it up like a leaf. She'd cried for weeks.

Now she had two new moonstones. Maybe these earrings would give her *new* power? They would be her seventh-grade lucky charms, for sure.

After they had cleaned up all the dishes, Madison started to tell Dad about everything she'd been doing on the new computer.

"I have these files, you see, so I can like, well, get my thoughts organized and all that. I think it's working so far. Of course it's only been two days."

Dad thought the file idea was fine. "As long as you don't have a 'Things I Hate About Dad' file," he joked.

Madison gasped. "Never! Daddy, of course I wouldn't."

Of course, Madison knew she should probably never say *never,* but she said it anyway. She couldn't imagine not liking her Dad. He was the one who always came to her rescue. He never said bad things about people. Even tonight, for a few hours, it was like he washed away all the yukkies of the previous few days. Madison found herself talking on and on about nothing at all and yet it all seemed so important, the way Dad listened. He was maybe the best listener in the entire world.

"Well, it's funny you should mention all that stuff about going on the computer, Madison, because . . ." Dad handed her a rather large box before he finished his thought. It wasn't wrapped or anything, just taped shut. "I have this for you, too."

"Daddy, what is *this*?" Madison was perplexed. She opened it and found herself face to face with a brand-new, high-resolution computer scanner. "No way!"

"I thought it would be a good thing for you to have. I know you have my old dinosaur of a scanner, but now you can scan and design all that new stuff. You can make screen savers, too. See, I stuck a photo of you and Phin right there. Put it up on your screen. I hope you like it, sweetheart."

Madison felt like crying. Daddy hadn't even really known about the files yet, but he was already on that wavelength. She was amazed at how Daddy always knew what to get, what to say, and what to do. Now the files of Madison Finn had *unlimited* possibilities.

Madison went on to tell Dad about her new friend Fiona and not-so-drippy-anymore Hart Jones and even Poison Ivy.

"Hey, Daddy, did I tell you that I think I'm also going to take a computer class with Egg this year?"

She and Dad swapped computer stories until they both noticed the clock. It was already ten.

Dad sighed. "Time flies when you're having . . ."

". . . dinner with the best dad on the planet," Madison finished his sentence.

Of course, Mom was expecting them back home a half-hour earlier. Madison pictured her out on the porch on Blueberry Street, playing tug-the-chew-toy with Phin, exhaling something not so nice about Dad under her breath. Mom hated when people were late more than anything else.

"We'd better go, Dad." Madison decided for the both of them.

When they arrived at the house, Daddy walked Madison as far as the front-door threshold and kissed her on the top of her head. He walked back to carry her computer scanner up from the car.

Madison liked it when Dad walked her up to the door. It made her feel safe. Of course, Phineas and Mom were waiting up on couch. Mom opened the door.

"Hello, Jeffrey," she said coldly. "Right on time, as usual."

Dad didn't seem to mind the chill. He jumped at the opening in the conversation. "Hello, Fran. I heard your trip to Brazil was a success? Hearty congratulations."

"Yes, well, we'll see you later, then." Mom looked at Madison and then walked back inside.

Madison tugged Dad's arm. "Thanks again,

Daddy. The earrings are cool and the new scanner is cooler than cool."

Through the living room bay window, Madison watched as Dad drove away. Rain started to pitter-pat against the sill. She pulled another one of Gramma's afghans over her toes and watched her breath on the cool glass.

Upstairs, Madison slid into her favorite Lisa Simpson T-shirt and sat down at her computer. She opened yet another new folder and named it.

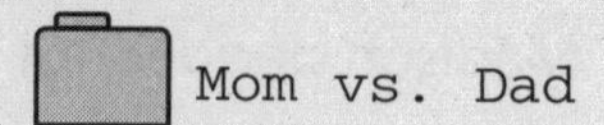

She certainly had a *lot* to say on this subject. Of course, it was all stuff she could never, ever say out loud. She wouldn't even tell Aimee some of this stuff—and she told Aimee absolutely everything. After the lists were typed, she returned to another file.

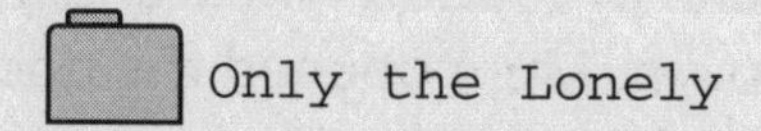

My school psychologist told me last year that I had to be patient. He told me I had to let Mom and Dad figure out their own lives again. So I am trying. Sometimes it's hard to imagine how two people could ever have let themselves get so mad at each other the way Mom and Dad did, but it happened and that's that I guess. I still keep their wedding picture on my file cabinet just because it makes me think of

when they were trying a little harder to be nice. They must have loved each other once, right?

I know I get mad at Aimee sometimes, but the truth is that she is still my best friend and I have to keep reminding myself of that fact. Besides, I can't be mad at my BFF just because she talks too much, can I? What qualifies as a good reason to stay mad at someone?

There are no reasons good enough to stay mad forever. I mean, if I wanted to be mad at anyone it would have to be Egg because he is the most obnoxious boy who ever lived, but the truth is I am NOT mad at Egg. For one thing, he always remembers my birthday and for another thing, he sticks up for me in gym class even when I can't make it on base in kickball.

Staying mad is a huge waste of time.

Some people have it so hard and my life is not that hard at all, even though I act like it is. What's so hard about this? I can handle it. I will handle it.

Tomorrow I will find Fiona.

I will find Fiona and I will say I'm sorry.

I will not let Poison Ivy or *anyone* get in my way.

Most of all, tomorrow I will stop obsessing about this lonely stuff once and for all. And even though my nickname just happens to be Maddie, tomorrow I will get un-mad.

Chapter 13

Science "block" in Room 411 felt more like cell block 411. The fourth day of school was practically over and Madison found herself alone again.

Mr. Danehy's class was a collection of people Madison wasn't sure she really wanted to be with.

Madison sat across from Poison Ivy, who was sitting next to the blond guy she'd been talking to in homeroom. Phony Joanie was across from him. Across the room, Madison caught Chet Waters picking his nose but he didn't seem to care about getting caught and in the back of the class Hart Jones had his attentions focused on a redheaded girl who Madison had never seen before. Plus, there was a bunch of other kids from her old middle school and the other middle

school in town scattered here, there, and everywhere.

"Hey, you were hanging with my sister, right?" Chet said.

Madison nodded and stuck her nose into her notebook.

It wasn't that people weren't *friendly*. Everyone was comparing summer tans and asking questions and Madison was in the mix. It was just that out of all the classrooms in all the schools in all the countries of the world, Poison Ivy and the others had walked into hers.

"Hey, Mad! Have you seen Walter?" piped a voice from behind

"My name is not *Mad*," she snapped back. But as soon as she turned, she realized that she had just snapped at Egg's friend Drew. "Oh, it's you."

Drew sighed, "No prob."

But Madison felt awful. "I didn't mean to yell, it's just that—"

"No prob," Drew repeated. "Really."

A kid from the back row yelled out, "Yo, Drew! Isn't your BBQ today?" and the entire class started buzzing. He'd invited the entire seventh grade section to his house for a barbecue—and *everyone* was planning to go.

Madison wondered how 300 people would fit into Drew's house. Did his mother know he'd overinvited by about 250 people? Madison figured the

reason for the massive invite list was simple: Drew was the kind of kid who couldn't say no to anyone. He didn't want anyone to feel left out.

After waiting past the second bell, the science teacher, Mr. Danehy, finally rushed into the room and quickly handed out a list of things they'd be studying.

"I am sorry to be late, class," he said "The copy machine busted down and I had to wait. How is everyone today? As you know, I'm Mr. Danehy."

The class was whispering like a chorus of crickets—about science, Mr. Danehy's ugly brown tie, and most of all about Drew's upcoming barbecue, which was scheduled to begin in less than three hours.

"Okay, now quiet down, please," Mr. Danehy said. "We need to get going since this period is going to be really short today."

Madison read the top of the page the teacher had passed out. The words *ozone*, *waste*, and *parasites* jumped out at her.

Sounds great, she thought. It's all dead stuff. What about living, breathing *animals*, Mr. Danehy—huh?

"In addition to the items on this page, we will also be dissecting a frog," Mr. Danehy announced. "A *virtual* frog."

Madison grimaced. *Virtual* frog? She didn't want to cut open anything, not even on a computer screen. What animal-lover Madison Finn really

wanted to study was penguins and puffins, as they had in third grade. Why couldn't they study arctic creatures all over again? Why couldn't she just be *in* third grade again, when life had been so much easier? In third grade, Madison didn't have to worry about enemies like Ivy. Everyone liked everyone else.

After the bell rang, Madison met up with Aimee at the lockers. They'd gotten their locker assignments in homeroom that morning.

"I saw your friend Fiona in class," Aimee said as soon as she saw Madison.

"You did? Where?" Madison couldn't believe Aimee had found Fiona today before she had.

"In our science block the teacher paired us up as lab partners. Pretty scary, huh, how things work out? She's cool though. We talked a lot."

Madison couldn't believe it. "Well, what did you talk about? What did she say? What happened?"

"What are you getting all worked up about?" Aimee snapped. "You new friend barely said anything except how nice you were and that you guys had fun over the summer. I asked her about that. What's the big deal, Madison?"

"Is she going to the barbecue today?" Madison asked. "What did you talk about?"

"Why don't you just ask her?" Aimee answered. "She's coming down the hallway right now."

Of course, what Aimee neglected to say was that Fiona was walking down the hallway with Poison Ivy, Rose *Thorn* and *Phony* Joanie.

Madison turned away.

"Madison!" Aimee poked her. "Fiona's coming right . . ."

But Madison's head was stuck into the locker, where she emptied her bookbag and stayed as still as she possibly could.

"Madison?" It was Fiona's voice calling her name this time, but Madison still didn't move.

Everything with Fiona was different now that they were in school. There was no way she could associate with Fiona and Ivy together. It wasn't the same as over the summer. Maybe they were meant to be summer friends and that was that. Madison Finn was cornered, so running away was out of the question. This time, she just froze.

After a few seconds, Fiona just walked away.

Ivy made a face at Aimee and blurted, "Nice friends you are."

Madison's stomach flip-flopped.

"What was *THAT*?" Aimee said as soon as Fiona and Ivy and the rest of the gang were gone. "Madison Finn, that was so strange. I don't think I have ever seen you blow someone off like that before. I can't believe she was standing there trying to talk and you just . . . *ignored* her? That is so mean. I can't believe—"

Madison finally interrupted her. "Just leave me alone, Aimee."

Aimee shook her head with disbelief. "Fine, be that way." And she walked away.

Madison ran into the girls' bathroom to cry. She felt sick and now she hated seventh grade more than before and it was only the FOURTH DAY! There was no way Fiona would ever talk to her again. Even Aimee was probably going to stay angry for a little while. Madison had started the day wanted to be everything but mad, and ended up alienating half her friends.

Drew saw her as she walked out of the bathroom.

"Madison, don't forget about the party," he said, handing her a slip of paper. On it he'd written, *BBQ Party at Drew's*. It had the address and phone number of his place.

But Madison just shoved it into her backpack and headed home—*alone.*

Since Mom was still off at work by the time Madison got back to Blueberry Street, she took her laptop out to the porch to wait around.

It was a beautiful sunny day. The clouds were practically invisible, just wisps of gauze across the blue sky. There was even a soft breeze in the air.

It was a perfect day for a barbecue.

Madison logged on to bigfishbowl.com almost immediately and was amazed to discover that

Bigwheels was online. She sent her an IM and arranged to meet in a "private" fishbowl.

<MadFinn>: help
<Bigwheels>: how was the first week of jr hi???
<MadFinn>: right now evryone is @ a bbq except me
<Bigwheels>: y??? y do u nd help?
<MadFinn>: I am all alone
<Bigwheels>: no ur not
<MadFinn>: yes didn't you read evry one is @ a party
<MadFinn>: except 4 me
<Bigwheels>: STOP
<MadFinn>: :-@!!!!!!!!!!!
<Bigwheels>: ic
<MadFinn>: :-@!!!!!!!!!!!
<Bigwheels>: quit screaming it can't be so bad
<MadFinn>: I am so stupid :'>(
<Bigwheels>: do u wanna talk ?
<MadFinn>: Y
<Bigwheels>: is that yes?
<MadFinn>: Y
<Bigwheels>: ok so were you not invited is that
<Bigwheels>: what the prob is????
<MadFinn>: nonnono
<Bigwheels>: ok so what???
<Bigwheels>: are u there?

<MadFinn>: Y
<MadFinn>: I am a loser
<Bigwheels>: ur a loser if u blow off the party YBS
<MadFinn>: YBS?
<Bigwheels>: You'll be sorry!
<MadFinn>: u think :~/
<Bigwheels>: look I dontknow u that well but here
<Bigwheels>: is the deal I think that ur just
<Bigwheels>: nervous about school startin we all r
<Bigwheels>: that way and u should be nice to
<Bigwheels>: ur friends NOT :~/
<MadFinn>: hw bout :-|
<Bigwheels>: LOL that's better
<MadFinn>: so I should go 2 the bbq???
<Bigwheels>: DTRT
<MadFinn>: ??????
<Bigwheels>: Do the right thing!
<MadFinn>: tx
<Bigwheels>: send me EMSG when u get home from the
<Bigwheels>: bbq GL
<MadFinn>: TTFN
<Bigwheels>: *poof*

Bigwheels had logged off and Madison did too.

She closed her laptop and went upstairs to pick out an outfit.

She had a barbecue to go to—and a lot of explaining to do.

Chapter 14

Madison had been staring at her reflection for at least ten minutes.

"Phin, what am I gonna wear?" she was hoping maybe the dog could tell her the best look for end-of-summer barbecues, but he was too busy sucking on a rawhide chewie to offer fashion advice.

Madison tried on the plaid jumper with her pink T-shirt. *Nope.* She looked sicker than sick in pink.

She tried on the blue striped tank with matching skort—a skirt-and-shorts outfit her mom had gotten for her last summer. *Skort? No self-respecting seventh grader would be caught dead in a skort!*

She tried on the yellow sundress from last night. *Too risky. What if Fiona had on her yellow sundress, too?*

Finally, Madison decided on denim shorts, a plain white T-shirt and sneakers. She pulled her hair up into her signature ponytails.

"Whaddya think, Phinnie?" she asked her pug. "Might as well call me Plain Jane, right?"

She did look a little boring, but maybe nondescript was a good way to sneak into the party, apologize to Fiona, have a few laughs with Aimee, Egg, and Drew, and sneak right back out again?

Madison dug her hand into her backpack and pulled out the slip of paper Drew had handed to her at school earlier. He lived all the way across town in Falstaff Fairway, a giant mansion with its own tennis court, pool, and a bunch of other stuff that cost a bunch of money. Drew's great-grandad had invented some little washer or screw or something that every single plumber in America and all over the world used in plumbing.

Translation: Drew's family were bazillionaires. Who else could host a barbecue for over 300 screaming twelve and thirteen year-olds?

Before dashing out the door, Madison applied a layer of Strawberry-Kiwi Smooch. She had no plans to kiss anyone at the party, but she wanted to look good. She figured that if she looked good, she'd feel good, and if she felt good, she'd do good.

Madison needed to do *real* good in order to get Fiona's forgiveness.

Then she put on her new moonstone earrings from Dad for good luck.

The bus ride over to Drew's place only took fifteen minutes. All the way up Drew's front walkway were different colored balloons. He even had orange balloons. Madison liked those the best.

Naturally, the entire Far Hills seventh-grade class *was* in attendance.

There were people in the pool (and lifeguards, too, thanks to Drew's parents).

Next to the pool, a dozen or more seventh-grade girls were lying out to get suntanned. Madison hadn't even brought her bathing suit.

A group of guys were playing Frisbee on the massive lawn.

Another group of guys were sitting in a semicircle checking out the seventh-grade girls who were sunbathing.

There were even a few people milling around who definitely looked like eighth graders.

There was, however, no immediate sign of Fiona or Aimee.

"Hey, yo!" Chet Waters said with a mouthful of potato chips. He walked over to Madison before she had a chance to escape.

"Hey, yo back!" she said.

"You seen Fi-moan-a around here?" he asked. "That Ivy girl was looking for her."

Madison frowned. "No."

"Did you come with Fiona?" Chet asked.

"No, didn't you?"

He shrugged "no" and walked away.

"Weirdo," Madison mumbled under her breath. She couldn't believe Chet and Fiona were twins. They may have looked alike, but they were total opposites.

Someone reached for Madison's arm. "So you came," a voice said softly.

It was Drew.

"Drew!" Madison turned. "What a party! Wow."

Madison had known Drew for years, but she'd never actually been to his place.

He nodded. "Thanks. I'm glad you came."

The music blared. There was a band in the middle of the yard and they were playing at top volume.

"I like your earrings," Drew said.

"What did you say?" Madison yelled.

Drew just smiled. "Cool earrings, Madison," he said again.

"What did you say?" Madison yelled louder. She leaned in closer "I can't hear."

"Great party." He nodded, and took a sip from his can of soda.

"Have you seen Aimee?" Madison asked, looking around for her BFF in the pool, on the lawn, on the patio.

"Inside," he answered. "Aimee's inside with Egg and that new girl, Fiona, I think."

Jackpot! Madison thanked Drew and headed into the house.

"Madison Finn?" Drew's mother greeted her as she walked through the sliders. "I haven't seen you since sixth-grade graduation!"

"Mrs. Maxwell! Thanks so much for inviting me to the party."

"Well, I'd say Drew outdid himself again, inviting the whole school, for goodness sake." She laughed and walked into the crowd. "Off I go! Have fun, my dear!"

Across the giant kitchen, Egg, Aimee, and Fiona were laughing.

Madison approached. At first, she could almost feel her sneakers turning to run in the opposite direction, but she resisted.

She moved *forward*.

"Maddie!" Egg screamed and slapped her on the shoulder. "How nice of you to come!"

Aimee just grunted "Hello." Whenever Aimee was even the littlest bit mad, it showed all over her face. Her lip curled, her nose wrinkled, and her eyes got all squinched up. She looked that way now.

Fiona just smiled. "Hi, Madison."

Everyone stood around for a few seconds in silence.

After ignoring Fiona in the lunchroom and turning her back to Fiona at the lockers, why wasn't Madison getting told off?

Aimee finally made a face. "Look, Fiona, you don't have to be nice to her just because we're standing here."

Egg chimed in. "No way! Let's be mean to Maddie! It's mad fun!"

Madison took a deep breath. Now she was going to get it.

"I really don't want to be mean to anyone," Fiona said. "I mean this was all some kind of weird misunderstanding, I think."

Madison felt so guilty. "Fiona, let me explain—"

"Madison, I don't expect to change everything in your entire universe just because we hung out for a little while this summer, right?"

Aimee made another face. "Are you for real?"

Fiona nodded. "Of course I'm for real, Aimee. Are you?"

"Whoooooo!" Egg shrieked.

Madison interjected. "Look you guys, I am so sorry. I don't want to hurt your feelings, Fiona. And of course I don't want to hurt yours either, Aimee."

Aimee huffed. "I know."

Madison added, "It was a misunderstanding, all of it. So can we just go back and start again?"

"Oh, get a room!" Egg cracked. "All this girl stuff makes me want to hurl. Where's Drew?"

Aimee crossed her arms a little tighter when Madison and Fiona leaned in to hug and make up. Madison hoped this hug wasn't fake. Like wrestling

was fake. She really wanted the three of them to be friends.

Egg put on a high-pitched girls voice. "What about *me*?"

Fiona laughed and teased. "What *about* you?"

Fiona was definitely flirting and Madison was weirded out. She remembered how Fiona had said Egg was a cutie.

Aimee put in her two cents. "Egg, you are such a dip. And you know where dips belong? With the chips!"

Fiona smiled. "I don't get it."

"You know, potato chips and dip, get it now?" Aimee said helpfully.

"Oh, sort of." Fiona grabbed Madison's arm. "Wanna play Frisbee?"

"Sure!" Madison grabbed Aimee's arm. "What about it, Aimee?"

"Yeah," Fiona said. "Come on, Aimee."

Madison looked at her friend as if to say, "Come on, let's just go play Frisbee and act stupid and forget about everything else today, okay?"

Aimee had other ideas. "Nah, you two go ahead."

"No," Madison said. "Aimee, we can't play without you."

Fiona tapped her foot. "Are we playing . . . or *staying*?"

Madison shook her head. "I think that I'll pass, Fiona."

Fiona shrugged and walked toward the lawn. "Okay. See you later then! Call me, okay?"

Madison nodded. "See you later!"

"You didn't have to not play just because of me," Aimee blurted out. "When I was at camp I was actually a good Frisbee player, but right now I just don't feel like it for some reason, but that doesn't mean you have to stop. I didn't mean to upset you or get in between you and Fiona and—I feel like a big doofus right now. Jeesh."

Madison grabbed Aimee's arm. "You're my BFF, Aimee. That means forever, remember. Who cares about Frisbee?"

They decided to go hang out by the pool instead.

Mom picked the Three Musketeers up sometime after ten o'clock, which was late, but okay because it wasn't a school night. Phin was in the car of course, and Egg teased him mercilessly all the way home.

"Dawg fooooooood!" he tickled Phin on his soft, spotted pug belly.

"Leave my dog alone!" Madison punched Egg right in the arm.

"Ouch! That hurt!" he yelled.

"Rowroooo!" Phin howled.

Mom dropped off Aimee last. She and Madison made a pact to see each other tomorrow, Saturday. It was supposed to get *really* hot.

Later that night, after Mom thought she had already turned out the light and left her daughter

in the land of Nod, Madison pulled her laptop computer into bed with her.

She owed Bigwheels a note.

From: MadFinn
To: Bigwheels
Subject: BBQ
Date: Fri 8 Sept 11:11 PM

I went. It was on this big estate and everyone was sunbathing and smiling and I waltzed in and made the friend thing work like you said I could.

Thank you for your long-distance advice.

I couldn't have BBQ-ed without you. You know if you ever need advice from me, I'll try to give it!

Yours till the root beer floats,
MadFinn

p.s. write back sooner than soon!

Lastly, Madison went into her favorite file.

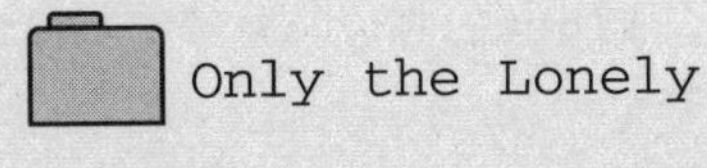
Only the Lonely

Today was Drew's BBQ.

He had one in fifth grade, the first one he ever threw I think, but I had a cold and had to stay home from school that day. He had one last year, too, but I can't remember exactly why I wasn't there. I seem to remember being in the middle of some kind of personal crisis seeing as that is the time when Mom and Dad got the big D. Yeah that was definitely it. The big D got in the way a lot last year.

All I can think about is the way things used to be and how that won't ever *change*. What I mean is that no one can ever take any of that away from me. No matter whatever happens in the future, I own every little thing that has already happened in the past—all the food fights, the pop quizzes, all of it.

Maybe worrying about being only the lonely was TOTALLY normal??? Maybe everyone is a bit lonely.

How can I possibly be lonely when everything that makes me and Aimee BFFs has already happened? No one can take that. So no matter how many Fionas I meet, no matter how my body changes, no matter how time flies, Aimee and I will never change what makes us close. No one can take away the soul sisters pact from fourth grade or the fact that I know all her secrets and she knows all of mine, right? Why is it that I can't ever seem to

Madison's eyes were getting very sleepy. She

tried to keep writing, but she just couldn't, so she turned off her computer and pulled up the blankets, patting the bed a few times so Phin would leap up and under the covers. Of course the dog jumped in immediately. He licked Madison's nose. That was his puggly way of saying nighty-night.

Madison had been afraid she wouldn't make it through the summer.

But she had—all the way through to September.

She was scared about starting seventh grade.

But here she was—and the giant pink welt on her shoulder had already disappeared.

She closed her tired eyes dreaming about how she and Aimee would spend Saturday afternoon tomorrow in the middle of the Indian summer heat wave, dancing in the sprinklers on Aimee's lawn, getting cooled off, and laughing the way they did every summer—just like last year and all the years before that.

From now on, Madison Finn would be only the lonely no more. She was ready to expect the unexpected.

Mad Chat Words:

:>)	Smile
(( ))*	Hugs and Smooches
:-@	I'm screaming!
;-)	Winky-wink
poof	Has left the chat room
GMTA	Great Minds Think Alike
IMO	In My Opinion
LOL	Laugh Out Loud
BTW	By the Way
L8R	Later
2K4W	Too Cool For Words
TTFN	Ta Ta For Now
BRB	Be Right Back

Madison's Computer Tip:

Whenever you are online, you have to be smart and safe, especially when you're in chat rooms. **Never give out information about you or your family online.** This means no phone numbers, addresses, passwords, or credit card numbers. I always tell my Mom or Dad where I surf online and who I talk to. You should too.

Visit Madison at www.madisonfinn.com

Take a sneak peek at the new

#2: Boy, Oh Boy!

Chapter 1

Fifteen minutes into the start of the school day, and Madison Finn had already chewed off all the orange glitter polish on her left hand. It was one of Madison's thirty or so nervous habits, right up there on the list next to sweating when she tried to play the flute and fleeing the scene when she was embarrassed. She was very skilled at fleeing.

Mrs. Wing stood in front of the classroom. "Welcome to the twenty-first century, where technology teacher and librarian morph into one being. Well, online librarian, anyhow. I'm your happy cybrarian, at your service."

"That's Mrs. Cybrarian to us, right?" Egg (a.k.a. Walter Diaz) said aloud, his voice warbling.

"Last week we talked about some basic facts about computers," Mrs. Wing said, lecturing from the front of the class. "We covered how hardware is assembled and how chips are made. And Mr. Diaz was kind enough to explain to us how a chip works."

She glanced over to Egg's desk and he grinned a real Grinchy grin.

"No prob', Mrs. Wing," he said.

Madison flared her nostrils. The only thing she hated more than Egg's constant crushing on teachers was when he was being extra cocky.

Ever since Madison and Egg were kids, he had crushed on pretty female teachers. First it was kindergarten's Miss Jeremiah; now it was the seventh-grade cybrarian.

Mrs. Wing fit into Egg's crush category perfectly. She was prettier than pretty, Madison thought to herself. Her long hair was swept up into a French twist and she wore a long plum-colored skirt, a neat white blouse, and a red-bead necklace. She moved around the room as if she were walking on cotton balls, floating from computer station to station, beads plink-plink-plinking together.

"Now, what I'd like to try out with the class this week are some basic programming skills," Mrs. Wing continued. "I think we're all ready to move ahead, am I right?"

Lance, a quiet kid who always sat at the back of the classroom, raised his hand and shook his head,

dejected. He didn't get computers and felt way left out. He was not ready. Not by a long jump. Or was it a shot put?

Madison shot Egg a glance, but, thankfully, Mrs. Wing said she'd explain it again later.

"Learning Basic," Mrs. Wing went on, "means that every one of you in this room will be able to program a computer. Just think about that. Think about what that could do for all of you. And looking around, I can see already that I have a classroom filled with technological geniuses . . . even you, Lance."

As soon as she said that, someone on the other side of the room snorted. Madison realized it was Egg's best friend, Drew Maxwell, who laughed as soon he heard the words Lance and genius uttered in the same breath. And as soon as he snorted, Egg snorted too. And then this kid PJ Rigby snorted. And then Jason Szelewski, Beth Dunfey, Suresh Dhir—everyone snorted.

It sounded like a pig farm.

Mrs. Wing didn't get mad though. She just sort of snorted right back.

"Well, I can see we'll be having a lot of fun in here, class. Just let's make sure it's not at someone else's expense, okay?"

Madison saw Egg making puppy-dog eyes at the back of Mrs. Wing's head when she said that. She turned away to reread her onscreen notes.

```
Dim strTemper As String
Const strNormNumbers$ = "0123456789"
Exit Function
End If
End If
OnlyNumericTextInput = strSource
End Function
```

After reviewing her page of code about strings and substrings and lots of little dollar signs, Madison popped in a disk and booted up her own personal file.

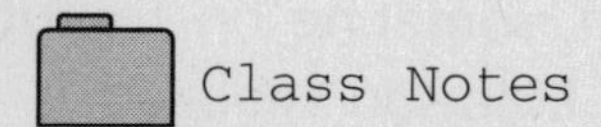

Nothing at Far Hills Junior High is what I expected. I thought it would be way different than middle school. NOT. I figured there was no way the same people from Far Hills Elementary would be geeks or popular, but that is just the way it is, like the same thing as last year but in a different building. Dad says I always over-think this kind of stuff, but it's just so hard to hold back a thought sometimes.

Mrs. Wing is sooo smart, so she probably will catch me right now writing personal stuff and not school stuff but oh well. She's all

the way on the other side of the room.

I like the way her beads look like red jelly beans. I wear a ring on almost every single finger, but I don't go for necklaces as much. Maybe I should?